THE LEGIO
FROM LONDINIUM

Caroline Lawrence is American. She grew up in California and came to England when she won a scholarship to Cambridge to study Classical Archaeology, which she followed with a degree in Hebrew and Jewish studies at the University of London. She lives by the river in London with her husband, a writer and graphic designer. In 2009, she was awarded the Classics Association Prize for 'a significant contribution to the public understanding of Classics.'

To find out more about the Roman Mysteries, visit www.romanmysteries.com

THE ROMAN MYSTERIES
by Caroline Lawrence

Also available:

—— A Roman Mystery ——

THE LEGIONARY FROM LONDINIUM AND OTHER MINI-MYSTERIES

Caroline Lawrence

Orion
Children's Books

First published in Great Britain in 2010
by Orion Children's Books
a division of the Orion Publishing Group Ltd
Orion House
5 Upper St Martin's Lane
London WC2H 9EA
An Hachette UK company

1 3 5 7 9 10 8 6 4 2

The Orion Publishing Group's policy is to use papers that are natural,
renewable and recyclable products and made from wood grown in sustainable
forests. The logging and manufacturing processes are expected to conform to
the environmental regulations of the country of origin.

A catalogue record for this book is
available from the British Library

ISBN 978 1 84255 192 9

Printed in Great Britain by Clays Ltd, St Ives plc

www.orionbooks.co.uk

To Otana Jakpor, 'fan number 27',
who helped me write one of these stories

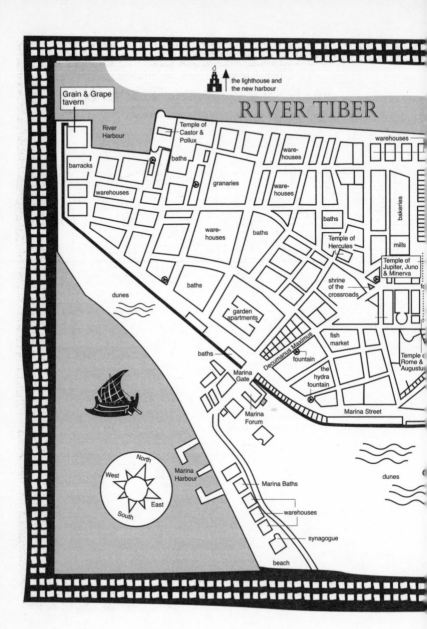

the lighthouse and
the new harbour

RIVER TIBER

Grain & Grape
tavern

River
Harbour

Temple of
Castor &
Pollux

warehouses

barracks

baths

ware-
houses

warehouses

granaries

ware-
houses

warehouses

baths

ware-
houses

baths

Temple of
Hercules

bakeries

mills

Temple of
Jupiter, Juno
& Minerva

dunes

baths

shrine
of the
crossroads

baths

garden
apartments

fish
market

Temple of
Rome &
Augustus

baths

Decumanus Maximus

fountain

Marina
Gate

the
hydra
fountain

Marina Street

Marina
Forum

North

West

Marina
Harbour

East

South

Marina Baths

dunes

warehouses

synagogue

beach

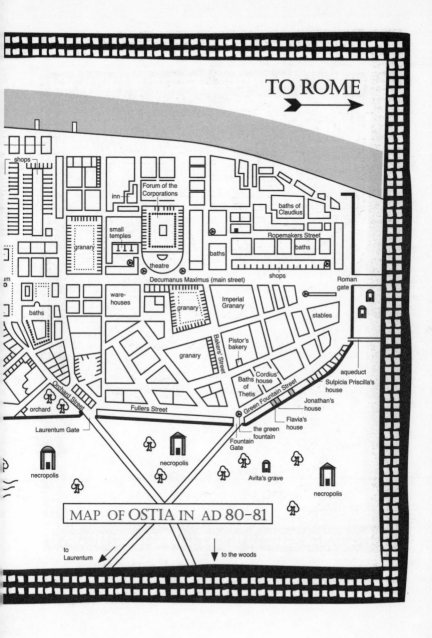

TO ROME

shops

inn

Forum of the Corporations

small temples

granary

theatre

baths of Claudius

Ropemakers Street

baths

baths

shops

Roman gate

Decumanus Maximus (main street)

ware-houses

granary

Imperial Granary

stables

baths

granary

Bakers' Street

Pistor's bakery

Baths of Thetis

Cordius' house

aqueduct

Sulpicia Priscilla's house

Green Fountain Street

Jonathan's house

orchard

Orchard Street

Fullers Street

Flavia's house

the green fountain

Laurentum Gate

Fountain Gate

necropolis

necropolis

Avita's grave

necropolis

MAP OF OSTIA IN AD 80-81

to Laurentum

to the woods

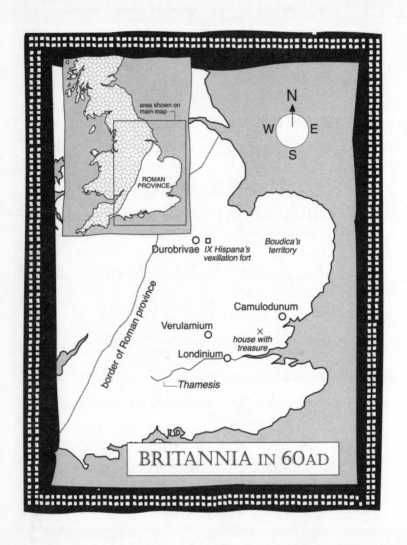

area shown on
main map

ROMAN
PROVINCE

N
W E
S

Durobrivae   IX Hispana's
vexillation fort

Boudica's
territory

Camulodunum

Verulamium

border of Roman province

house with
treasure

Londinium

Thamesis

BRITANNIA IN 60AD

CONTENTS

INTRODUCTION

by Caroline Lawrence

From *The Thieves of Ostia* to *The Man from Pomegranate Street*, there are seventeen books in the Roman Mysteries series. Originally I planned to write eighteen, but I had to scratch a title off my list. In the abandoned book, I was going to send Flavia and her friends to solve a mystery in Roman Britain. But because my books take place around real historical events, I was running out of time. Book sixteen finds the four friends in Ephesus in August AD 81, for events crucial to the arc of the series. The final mystery was always going to be about the sudden death of Titus in the Sabine Hills on the Ides of September in AD 81. That was going to be book number eighteen.

However, there was no way I could get my four young detectives from Ephesus (modern Turkey) to Britannia (Great Britain) and then back to Sabina (in Italy) in a month. So I had to scrap the idea of taking my friends to Roman Britain. The final Roman Mystery, *The Man from Pomegranate Street*, thus became number seventeen.

But British readers kept asking me when I would write a mystery set in Roman Britain. I found the solution while reading some Sherlock Holmes mystery stories. In one of these, Holmes solves a mystery originating in America without ever leaving London. That gave me the idea that Flavia could solve a mystery set in Britannia, but without leaving Ostia. She would use her imagination to solve the crime, just as she did in 'The Case of the Missing Coin' in the first volume of short stories: *Trimalchio's Feast and Other Mini-Mysteries.*

As with that first collection of short stories about Flavia and her friends, this volume contains stories which fill in some of the gaps between the full-length books. For example, in *The Man from Pomegranate Street*, Flavia seems to know how to treat the sting of a certain creature. How does she know this? We find out in one of the mini-mysteries in this collection

The very last mini-mystery is set after the final book of the Roman Mysteries, and it introduces a new detective for younger readers. For older readers I hope to write *The Flavian Trilogy*, set fourteen years on from the last Roman Mystery. These books would have adventure and mystery, but also love and passion.

Caroline Lawrence

These mini-mysteries take place in Ancient Roman times, so a few of the words may look strange.

If you don't know them, 'Aristo's Scroll' on pages 155–170 will tell you what they mean and how to pronounce them.

THE MOON IN
FULL DAYLIGHT

**This story takes place on the next to last
day of June in AD 80 (shortly after the events
of book XI, *The Sirens of Surrentum*)**

One hot summer morning, Flavia Gemina was coming back home from the forum when the sight of the moon stopped her short. It was almond shaped, hanging above the red-tiled roofs of Ostia like the unblinking eye of the goddess Diana. It was pearly and pale but perfectly distinct.

'What is wrong?' Nubia stopped beside the green marble fountain which gave their street its name.

'The moon,' said Flavia, 'in full daylight.'

'Yes,' said Nubia. 'Have you never seen this before?'

'I suppose I have,' said Flavia. 'But it's strange the way I suddenly saw it where the sky seemed empty a moment before. Of course the sky wasn't empty,' she added. 'The moon was there all along. I just didn't notice it.'

Both girls gazed up into the blue sky.

'I wonder if it's an omen,' murmured Flavia, and they both made the sign against evil.

Suddenly Nubia said: 'Hark! Do you hear that noise?'

Flavia listened. Above the splashing of the fountain and the chirring of the cicadas, she could hear something. 'Yes!' she breathed. 'It's coming from behind the fountain.'

Cautiously, she led the way around to the far side of the green fountain.

3

'Behold!' said Nubia, her golden-brown eyes growing wide.

A little boy of about four was sitting on the hard paving stones and crying.

'What's wrong?' Flavia asked him.

Nubia sat down beside him. 'Are you all right?'

The little boy looked up at them with wet black eyes.

'Where's your mother?' asked Flavia. 'Or your bodyguard?'

'Where do you live?' asked Nubia.

The boy blinked back at them. 'I want my mater!' His voice was barely audible.

'Where is your house?' asked Nubia gently.

'I don't know.' He was trembling.

'Is it on this street?' asked Flavia, gesturing up Green Fountain Street.

The boy shook his head, and whimpered. Fresh tears filled his eyes.

Nubia tried a different approach. 'I am Nubia,' she said gently. 'And this is Flavia Gemina. What is your name?'

'Postumus.' The tears spilled over.

Flavia could tell from the boy's cream linen tunic and good-quality sandals that he was highborn.

'What are your other two names?' asked Flavia, crouching down beside Nubia.

'I don't remember,' sniffed Postumus.

4

'Then can you tell me your father's name?'

'Pater.'

Flavia glanced at Nubia and gave a deep sigh.

'What does your father do?' she asked. 'For a living, I mean?'

'He kills things.'

The girls looked at each other in alarm. But before Flavia could ask him what sort of things his father killed, the boy clutched his stomach and curled up in a ball. 'My tummy hurts,' he whimpered.

'Let's get him to Doctor Mordecai,' said Flavia, and Nubia nodded.

A few moments later they were pounding on the door of the house next to theirs. Above the green door hung a bronze bleeding-cup; it showed that a doctor lived and practiced there. Flavia heard the welcome sound of Tigris barking, and a moment later Jonathan opened the door.

'Jonathan!' cried Flavia. 'We found this little boy crying behind the fountain. Something's wrong with him. Is your father here?'

'He's gone to see one of his patients,' said Jonathan, stepping back from the doorway and pulling Tigris away from Postumus. 'But come in. I'll have a look at him. Lupus and I were just about to go fishing,' he added, as Lupus came into the atrium with a net over his shoulder.

'Lupus!' said Flavia. 'Do you know this little boy?

Have you seen him before?'

Lupus shrugged and shook his head. Suddenly, he pointed at the boy and opened his eyes in alarm.

Flavia glanced down at Postumus. 'Great Juno's peacock!' she cried. 'He's foaming at the mouth!'

'I am seeing that on horses, but never on people,' murmured Nubia.

'He must have been poisoned,' said Jonathan.

'Maybe he was eating herbs in the necropolis,' said Nubia. 'Without knowing what they were.'

'We need to give him the antidote!' said Flavia. 'Quickly!'

'First,' said Jonathan, 'we need to know what poison he took or what plant he ate from. There are different antidotes for different poisons. Bring him into Father's study.'

Nubia picked up the shivering little boy, carried him into Mordecai's tablinum and laid him on the orange and red striped divan.

Jonathan took a sea sponge from his father's desk and handed it to Nubia. She gently wiped the boy's mouth with it.

'What are his symptoms?' said Jonathan, opening a wax tablet.

'Foaming at the mouth,' said Nubia.

'Nausea,' said Flavia, as the boy whimpered and clutched his stomach.

'He is shivering,' said Nubia, 'even though it is being very hot today.'

Lupus grunted to get their attention. He pointed at his own eyes, then at the boy's.

'Yes,' said Nubia. 'Behold, the black part of his eye is very big.'

'Dilated pupils,' muttered Jonathan, writing on the tablet. 'Nausea, shivering and foaming mouth.' He put down the wax tablet, took a scroll from a sturdy cylindrical basket on the floor and unrolled it on the desk.

Nubia gently wiped the little boy's mouth. 'Postumus, were you tasting of a plant or herb? Maybe some berries?'

He shook his head.

'Have you had anything to drink or eat recently?' Flavia asked the boy.

Postumus nodded and tried to speak, but his voice was now so faint that Flavia could not make out the words.

Flavia looked at Jonathan. 'Loss of voice,' she said grimly. 'Add that to your list of symptoms.'

Nubia brought her ear close to Postumus' mouth. She listened for a moment and shook her head. Then she frowned. 'His breath is smelling green,' she said. 'And also a little like blackberries.'

Flavia sniffed the boy's breath and then said,

'Postumus, are you sure you haven't eaten any berries today?'

The boy shook his head, and whimpered.

'Eureka!' cried Jonathan, looking up from the scroll. 'I think he's been poisoned by belladonna. Also known as Atropos, after one of the three Fates.'

Flavia nodded and said to Nubia. 'Atropos is the most deadly of the Three Fates. She is the one who cuts the Thread of Life, and she won't be turned aside. That's why she's called Atropos. It means "cannot be turned" in Greek.'

'I think I am knowing this plant,' said Nubia. 'It has dark blue berries.'

'Yes,' said Jonathan. 'Do you remember we researched it when we were in Surrentum? Although belladonna is highly poisonous, sometimes women bathe their eyes in a concoction of it to make their pupils bigger.'

Lupus grunted, raised his shoulders and turned his palms up: his gesture for Why?

Jonathan shrugged. 'Apparently,' he said, 'dilated pupils make you look more beautiful.'

Lupus shook his head in wonder.

'According to this,' continued Jonathan, 'a concoction of belladonnna is also drunk by some priests to induce a trance, and it can be used as a mouthwash against loose teeth.'

'But what's the antidote?' cried Flavia. Little Postumus had drawn his knees up to his chest and was shivering so much that his teeth were chattering.

Jonathan read: 'Swallow a large beaker of warm vinegar or mustard diluted in water to induce vomiting. Then, keep patient warm and still in a dark and quiet room.'

'Quickly!' cried Flavia, but Lupus had already hurried out of the tablinum.

A short time later he was back with a large copper beaker full of warm vinegar.

Nubia took the beaker from Lupus and encouraged little Postumus to drink. After one sip he turned his face away, but Nubia gently persisted.

'You must drink it all, Postumus,' said Flavia. 'Otherwise you could die.'

Little Postumus whimpered again as they made him drink.

'I'd better get a bucket,' said Jonathan, and hurried out of the room. He returned just in time. Postumus leant forward and vomited into the bucket.

Nubia took the sea-sponge, dipped it in the last of the vinegar water and gently wiped Postumus's face and mouth.

The little boy retched again and Nubia gently held his head. Finally Postumus curled up on the couch, exhausted and pale.

'Let's leave him there on the divan,' said Jonathan.

'It's quiet in here, and if I close the curtain it will be dim. I'll go and get some blankets.' He hurried out of the room.

Nubia stroked Postumus' forehead with the cool sponge, and spoke softly to him. Flavia watched her former slave-girl with admiration: Nubia was so good with children.

'His parents must be vexed,' said Nubia presently. 'Not knowing where he is.'

'Nubia's right,' said Jonathan, coming back into the tablinum with two blankets. 'They'll be sick with worry. We should find them as soon as possible.'

'But we don't know who they are,' said Flavia. 'Unless . . . Wait!' She held up her hand. 'Before you cover him, let me examine him for clues.'

Jonathan obediently waited as Flavia started by scrutinizing Postumus' feet. 'Nice leather sandals,' she said. 'But I don't recognise the maker's mark on the bottom. Maybe they're from Rome. High quality linen tunic,' she murmured, as she worked her way up. 'His family is definitely rich. No belt pouch or rings, but maybe– Eureka!' She pulled a bulla out from under the neck of his tunic. It was an amulet on a thong, a hollow gold ball about the size of a chestnut. It had a tiny hinge and when she finally opened it, a signet ring fell out.

'It's a man's ring,' said Flavia, 'Sardonyx in an iron setting.'

'What's the intaglio?' asked Jonathan, bending forward.

Nubia frowned. 'What is in tag low?'

'An intaglio,' said Flavia, 'is the carving in the gem of a signet ring. In this case a tiny club.' She looked at Nubia. 'The club is a symbol of—'

'Hercules!' said Nubia.

'Yes.'

'Lots of sailors worship Hercules,' said Jonathan.

Lupus nodded his agreement.

'That doesn't really narrow it down,' said Flavia with a sigh. 'Half the families in Ostia worship Hercules. In fact, there was something going on at his temple earlier today. Nubia and I saw the smoke rising up from the altar.'

Nubia looked at Jonathan and held out her hand for the blankets. 'Now we must be covering him, to warm him.'

Jonathan nodded and began to spread the blankets over Postumus. Nubia helped tuck them around the shivering boy.

Lupus had been writing something on his wax tablet. Now he showed it to them.

Flavia nodded. 'Good idea: let's see if anyone recognises the ring. It's nearly noon and people will be going to the baths soon,' she said. 'One of us can stand by the entrance of the Forum Baths and see if anyone knows who owns this ring.'

'I should stay here,' said Jonathan. 'I can keep an eye on our patient and explain the situation to Father, when he returns.' He went to the desk, took a piece of charcoal and began to write something on a piece of papyrus.

'I will stay with Postumus,' said Nubia, brushing a few damp strands of dark hair from the little boy's forehead.

'I'd better stay, too,' said Flavia. 'In case he recovers his voice and utters an important clue.'

Lupus grinned and raised his hand, as if to say: 'I'll go.'

'Well done, Lupus,' said Flavia.

'Here,' said Jonathan, handing the papyrus to Lupus. 'Before you go to the baths, put this up on the notice board in the forum.'

Lupus held it up, and Flavia read out loud:

FOUND: POSTUMUS, AGED ABOUT FOUR.
IF YOU HAVE LOST HIM, COME TO
THE HOUSE OF DOCTOR MORDECAI
ON GREEN FOUNTAIN STREET

'Good,' she said. 'That's good.'

After Lupus left, Flavia quietly pulled the curtain across the wide doorway of Mordecai's study, in order to keep out the bright sunlight. She turned and looked around. The room was dim now, and quiet. It

12

smelled strongly of medicinal herbs and faintly of vomit. She looked at Jonathan. Seen from behind, bending over the desk, he reminded her of his father. Lupus's fishing net lay on the floor where he had dropped it. As she bent to pick it up, she remembered that his father had been a fisherman on the Greek island of Symi. She put the net on the divan and went to sit near Nubia. Postumus was still pale, but shivering a little less. Nubia was tending him as gently as a mother would her own son.

Suddenly Flavia had the answer. She knew how the boy had been poisoned. It had been there all along, like the moon in the sky. But until now she hadn't seen it.

Jonathan looked up as she ran back to the curtain and pulled it open.

'What is it?' he asked, as bright daylight flooded the room.

'I think I have the answer!' she cried. 'If I can just catch Lupus we'll know soon enough.'

Half an hour later, they heard Tigris's bark echo in the atrium. Flavia followed Jonathan out of the tablinum. He pulled back the bolt and opened the front door to reveal the culprit: the very person Flavia had suspected.

It was a tall man in a priest's robes. He stood beside Lupus.

'I am Postumus Fulvius Salvis,' said the man. 'Chief

priest and haruspex at the Temple of Hercules.' He gestured at Lupus. 'This boy showed me a message on a wax tablet. It says you have found my son.'

'First,' said Flavia. 'We need to make sure you're really his father. Can you tell us what your son was wearing around his neck?'

'Why a bulla, of course,' said the priest impatiently. 'With one of my signet rings inside.' He showed Flavia an amethyst ring on his right hand. A small club of Hercules was carved into the purple stone.

'He's in the tablinum,' said Flavia, and turned to lead the way.

'Praise Hercules!' cried the priest, and rushed forward to embrace little Postumus. 'My wife is beside herself.'

'Shhh!' whispered Nubia. 'He was very ill but now he is asleep.'

'He was poisoned,' said Jonathan.

'What?' cried the priest, his eyes large and dark. 'Who would do such a thing?'

Flavia pointed her finger accusingly: 'You!'

'Impudent girl! How dare you accuse me of such a thing!'

'Earlier today, you drank a concoction of belladonna to put yourself into a trance, didn't you?'

'Yes ... but how did you know?'

'Because belladonna is what poisoned your son,' said Jonathan.

Lupus mimed someone drinking.

'But I always put the goblet back on the highest shelf,' said Salvis.

Nubia shook her head. 'I think this time you were leaving cup on table.'

'But I . . . perhaps I forgot to put it away. I was late for the ceremony and—'

'You were in too much of a hurry to put away the goblet, or to close the front door properly,' said Flavia. 'Or perhaps you were already confused by the belladonna. Anyway, after you left, your little boy drank the dregs from the goblet.'

'But why would he do that?' cried the priest.

'Because he wants to be like you,' said Flavia. 'Children often imitate their parents. Especially when they're little.'

'After he drank it,' said Jonathan, 'he probably began to hallucinate and somehow wandered out of the house, through the open front door.'

The priest tugged his dark hair. 'Dear gods! What have I done?'

'You should always keep dangerous brews and potions out of children's reach,' said Jonathan.

'And keep doors shut,' added Nubia gently.

The priest hung his head and nodded.

'If Nubia hadn't heard Postumus crying behind the fountain,' said Flavia, 'we might have walked right past him.'

'And your son would probably be dead by now,' said Jonathan.

'And if Flavia had not stopped to look at the moon,' added Nubia. 'I would not have been hearing him.'

'Yes,' said Flavia, and nodded wisely. 'If I were you, I'd give a thanks-offering to the goddess Diana. Today the moon helped save your son's life. The moon in full daylight.'

— AUTHOR'S NOTE —

I live in London, by the River Thames. I love walking around London. I often walk by the river, or up the Kings Road, or through one of London's many parks.

Sometimes when I am walking, I notice the moon in full daylight. The strange thing is: I might have been walking for twenty minutes or more before I notice it. It was there all along; I just didn't see it. One day this happened and the idea occurred to me that the moon in daylight is like the solution to a problem or a clue to a mystery. It was there all along, but you just didn't notice it. That gave me the idea for this short story.

THE LEGIONARY
FROM
LONDINIUM

This mystery takes place on the Nones of July
AD 80 after *The Sirens of Surrentum*

Flavia Gemina to her dear friend Polla Pulchra –

How wonderful it was to get your letter! I had been meaning to write to you, as we promised we would, but you were first across the line. Your prize shall be a long letter from me: this one!

I'm so glad that your mother is well and that you and your sisters are enjoying lessons with her. Yes, I know some of the Greek myths are 'quite horrid', but it is worth persisting. Let me tell you how my knowledge of the Greek myths helped me solve a mystery last week.

It was a blazing hot afternoon and I was reading my scroll of Apollodorus' Greek Myths in the shade of the fig tree by the fountain in the centre of our inner garden. Nubia was out in the graveyard with the boys, walking the dogs. Pater is on one of his voyages again so apart from the slaves, I was alone.

Suddenly, a pounding on the door made me almost jump out of my tunic. Who could be calling at siesta time?

A few moments later Caudex showed a man into the garden.

The stranger was quite tall and he stood very stiff and straight, like a legionary at attention. He was not wearing armour, however, just a plain tunic and those heavy sandals that soldiers and vigiles wear. He had thinning grey hair and bushy black eyebrows.

'Salve,' I said, putting my scroll down on the bench.

'Salve, young lady!' he said. 'Are you Flavia Gemina?'

I stood up. 'Yes, I'm Flavia. But I'm afraid my father isn't here. He's on a voyage.'

'As I told your door-slave, it's you I've come to see, not your father. My name is Probus, Marcus Favonius Probus. I need your help with a mystery.'

'A mystery?' My heart skipped a beat with excitement.

'Yes,' he said, coming to stand under the shade of the fig tree. 'Last year you helped my neighbour's daughter Pandora find a gold coin she'd lost.'

'I remember! How is Pandora?'

Probus shrugged. 'Fine, I suppose. Her father told me you found the coin without even going into her room.' He stroked a red mark under his chin with the knuckle of his right forefinger. 'But now that I see how young you are, I'm not sure you can help.'

'I'm not young,' I said, drawing myself up to my full height. 'I'm eleven years old. Next year I'll be of marriageable age.' I clapped my hands. 'Alma!' I called, in my most grown-up voice. 'Bring us two beakers of posca.' I turned back to Probus. 'You're used to posca, aren't you, sir? After all, you did serve in the army.'

'Great Jupiter's eyebrows!' he exclaimed. 'How in Hades did you know that? Did Pandora's father tell you I was coming?'

'No. I've never even met him and I haven't seen Pandora in ages. But I can tell you're a soldier by the way you stand, very stiff and straight. Although you're wearing a light summer tunic you have caligae on your feet. You have a muscular neck and a mark underneath your chin, probably caused by the chinstrap of a helmet, worn for years and years.'

'Great Jupiter's eyebrows!' He touched the mark with the knuckle of his right forefinger and now that I was closer I saw one of the rings he wore.

'You're quite old,' I continued bluntly, 'between forty and forty-five, so you're probably retired. Furthermore, I believe you used to serve with the Ninth Legion.'

'Great Jupiter's eyebrows!' he exclaimed for a third time. 'How did you know that?'

'Your signet ring,' I said. 'I can see the letters LEG VIIII HISP engraved on it.'

He chuckled. 'Very clever. And observant.' He gave me a keen look. 'Perhaps you can help me after all.'

I resisted the temptation to jump up and down with excitement. Instead, I tried to stay calm and businesslike. 'I can try,' I said. 'Please. Won't you sit?'

'I believe I will.'

I quickly moved the open scroll of Apollodorus and rolled it up as he sat on one end of the bench. I sat at the other end of the bench – which is semi-circular – so that we were facing each other. I put down Apollodorus and as I was taking my wax tablet from my belt pouch, Alma appeared with two beakers of posca. Probus took his and sipped it gratefully.

I thanked Alma and turned to the ex-legionary. 'So tell me, sir,' I said, opening my wax tablet. 'What is your mystery?'

'It's not unlike Pandora's,' he said, putting his beaker down. 'I need to find something that's hidden. Only it's not a single gold coin, it's a whole treasure trove. Gold coins, silver plate and jewelry. And it's not in a room here in Ostia. It's a thousand miles away, in the province of Britannia.'

'Where you served as a legionary?'

'Precisely. I served in Britannia for many years with the Ninth Hispana. After the rebellion, I was assigned to be a bodyguard of the governor in Londinium. Lived there for eighteen years. When I retired I came back here to Ostia. Brought my wife with me. Lovely girl from Calleva Atrebatum. Grey eyes like yours, but lighter hair.'

I took a leap of intuition. 'I'm sorry for your loss.'

He looked at me in astonishment and I knew my guess was right.

'Why do you say that?' he stammered.

'Your wife is dead, isn't she?'

'Yes, but how in Hades?'

I pointed with my stylus. 'Your tunic,' I said. 'There's a small rip in the shoulder seam and also a brown stain near the belt. It looks like fish-sauce. A wife would notice something like that and tell your body slave to put out a fresh tunic. Also, your eyes look sad.'

He swallowed and turned his head to look at the fountain. He was blinking away tears. 'My wife became ill after we arrived here,' he said. 'I spent all my money on doctors. The last of my savings went on her tomb. I didn't need the treasure before, but now I do.'

I could see he was embarrassed to admit these things to me, so I said: 'Tell me about the treasure.'

'It was during the rebellion of Boudica,' he said.

'Oh! I've heard of her,' I cried. 'Wasn't she the fierce warrior queen who led her people against the Romans living there? Six feet tall and armed like a man but with blazing red hair that came down to her waist?'

'So they say. I only saw her once, from a distance. Couldn't really see her hair or how tall she was. After she sacked and burnt Camulodunum – and

25

destroyed our infantry – our commander sent some of us ahead to warn Roman settlers and traders about her marauding army. That's when my friend helped one of the settlers hide a vast treasure.'

'Wait, sir,' I said. 'Can you start at the beginning? I'm confused.'

(You must always ask people to explain things you don't understand, Pulchra. It's far better than pretending you know something when you don't.)

'Beginning? Very well.' Probus stroked the callous beneath his chin. 'I was stationed at a vexillation fortress near Durobrivae.'

'What's a vexillation fortress?'

'A fortress that houses half a legion. There were five cohorts of legionaries at Durobrivae, and a cohort of auxiliaries. Legionaries are soldiers who are Roman citizens and auxiliaries are from other countries.'

'I do know that much.'

'Good. My friends and I were in the legionary cavalry. There are always a few horsemen attached to each infantry cohort, you see, to take messages and scout and the like. We were often on patrol, because the fort was situated on the border of three different tribes. They have tribes in Britain you know, each with different customs. Some tribes tattoo themselves, others paint themselves blue, some even allow women to lead them. Many Britons have red

26

hair, like Boudica. Or fair hair, like my dear wife.' He took another sip of posca. 'The rebellion occurred just over twenty years ago. It all started with an unfortunate incident among the tribe called the Iceni. Some Roman officials did things they shouldn't have. This was soon followed by rumours of unrest and terrifying omens.'

'Omens?' I said.

'Yes. For instance, at Camulodunum—'

'Where?'

'Camulodunum. Town near the coast. It's where our troops were first based when the Emperor Claudius invaded thirty years ago. Camulodunum became the first Roman Colony in Britannia.'

He stood up and used the toe of his caliga to draw a long blobby outline in the pebbled path. It looked like one of my omelettes gone wrong. Then he put a dark pebble on the lower part of the outline. 'That's Camulodunum,' he said. 'Our fort was here at Durobrivae.' He put another pebble above it and to the left. Then he put a third pebble underneath them both. 'The biggest town, Londinium, is down here at the first crossing place on their great river Thamesis.' He used a twig to draw the river. 'And the house with the treasure was here. Halfway between Camulodunum and Londinium.' He marked this spot with an X.

'Oh,' I said. 'So all those places you're talking

about are down there in the bottom corner of Britannia, on the right?'

'That's correct. The southeast. Now, where was I?'

'Omens in that town with a long name.' I pointed at the first pebble he had put down.

'Camulodunum,' he said, sitting down again. 'One day, for no reason the statue of Victory turned as if to flee, and fell on her face.'

Despite the heat of the afternoon, I shivered and made the sign against evil.

'Some also say that a ruined city was seen at the mouth of the Thamesis and that the sea turned to blood. Just as worrying were the rumours of native unrest. There was only a small military force at Camulodunum, you see, but many colonists. So they sent a message to the procurator, a fool named Decianus, asking for troops to protect them.'

Probus drained his beaker and put it down on the bench.

'Decianus did not believe there was any real threat, so he only sent two hundred men. When Boudica and her hoards attacked Camulodunum, those two hundred soldiers were the only force protecting the town, along with the discharged veterans who lived there. Word was brought to us and our commander Cerialis mobilized us at once.'

Probus mopped his face with his handkerchief. 'It was a slaughter. Boudica and her warriors didn't just

28

kill our soldiers, but civilians, too. Men, women and children.'

'Women and children, too?' I gasped. 'But why?'

'Because of an incident.' He glanced up at me. 'Some Romans whipped Boudica and abused her two daughters.'

'Oh how horrible. So you weren't in time to save the colonists?'

'No. We ourselves were ambushed as we hurried there.' Probus's tanned face had turned a ghastly pale.

'Sir, are you all right?' I asked.

'Do you have any wine?'

'Alma!' I directed my voice towards the kitchen. 'Can you bring us some wine and water?' Then I turned back to him. 'I often take deep breaths,' I said, 'when I feel sick.'

He nodded and did so. In the silence I could hear the fountain splashing and the cicadas throbbing while the swooping swifts in the sky above uttered their piercing cries.

Soon Alma came up to us with two silver pitchers on a tray. Before she could set it down on the bench between us, Probus grabbed the smaller pitcher and poured some wine into his beaker. I noticed his hand was shaking. He drank the wine down neat, without even watering it, then wiped his mouth with the back of his forearm.

'Boudica's army went through our infantry like a scythe through ripe wheat,' he said. 'Terrible carnage.'

'Oh!' I exclaimed again. 'Those poor men.'

He poured a second beaker of wine. 'Those of us with horses managed to escape. Including Cerialis, our leader. He headed back to our fortress but he sent some of us ahead to warn settlers and traders on the road south to Londinium.'

'Were you able to warn people?' I asked.

'A few.' He drained his second beaker of neat wine. 'Boudica's barbarians left the round huts untouched but they slaughtered anyone in a square or rectangular house.'

'Why?'

'Round huts meant natives, you see. Native Britons, that is. We Romans introduced straight walls and right angles to Britannia. Boudica's rabble knew anyone living in a straight house was either Roman or sympathetic to Rome. That was when I saw up close how Boudica's men tortured and mutilated their victims. I'll never forget the smell of roasting human flesh. Like pork, it was.'

In the hot blue sky above us, the swifts shrieked, as if with horror at what he was saying. I felt a little sick, too, so I took a few deep breaths and drank some of my posca. Vinegar always makes an upset stomach feel better.

'Go on,' I said.

'We were too late to help most of the settlers, but my friend Virgil and I were able to warn a few.'

'Virgil?' I said. 'Your friend was called Virgil? Like the poet?'

'Yes. His real name was Rufus, but everyone called him Virgil because he was always reading poetry. Composing it, too. On the second day of our scouting expedition,' continued Probus, 'Virgil and I found one villa untouched. It was hidden from the road by thick trees on the bank of a river. The owner was a Greek named Stephanos. Wife was a Briton and his sons both had red hair like her. I suppose he thought having a local girl for a wife might save him. But he lived in a rectangular house with mosaics and frescoes, and a two-columned porch. We told him to get out fast and only take the basics in case they encountered Boudica's marauders. We warned the man to stay quiet and let his wife do the talking. Urged him to go right away.'

'Did he?'

'Not straight away. He told us he had a lot of gold, silver and jewels. Made his fortune importing fish-sauce in Londinium, and then moved out to live in the country near his wife's people. He showed us his savings: a little bronze casket full of gold coins, silver cups and jewels. Virgil said the best plan would be to hide the treasure in the house, then recover it when he returned. That's what we advised most settlers we met who were still alive. Stephanos agreed and asked Virgil to help him. Meanwhile, I went out back to help the wife and sons load the cart.'

'Didn't the house have an inner garden or courtyard?' I asked.

'Not at that time,' he said. 'It was just a simple corridor house. That is to say, a long corridor along the front led off into different rooms.'

Probus looked better now. He poured himself some more wine but this time he added water. 'Half an hour later,' he said, 'we saw them off along the road to Londinium. As they drove away, we heard the thunder of horse's hooves and of marching feet. Boudica's army was approaching. We had to get out fast, too. As we mounted our horses and rode south, Virgil said if we ever grew poor we could always come back and get the treasure. If Stephanos and his family didn't survive to reclaim it themselves, that is.'

'And Virgil wouldn't tell you where he and Stephanos hid the treasure?'

'No.'

'Why not?'

'I suppose he thought I might come back later and keep in all for myself.' Probus absent-mindedly stroked the callous beneath his chin and looked at me. 'But I think he gave me a clue. When he was dying.'

'He died? Virgil died?'

Probus nodded. 'He died a few weeks later in the final battle against Boudica. Spoke his last words in the meter of those epic poems he was always composing. Like Homer and Virgil.'

'Dactylic hexameter?' I asked.

'Or something like it.'

'That's strange.'

'Indeed. We all thought he was delirious with pain.'

'What did he say?'

'He said, "I repent! I repent! Oh, a flute is not worth so great a price!"'

'Oh! I know that verse! I've just read it recently!'

'You mean he didn't make it up?' Probus leapt to his feet and stared down at me, his fists clenching and unclenching in excitement. 'By the gods! All these years I thought it was something he himself composed. Where is it from? The Aeneid?'

'I don't think so,' I said, 'It's from something I was reading recently ... do you think it could have been a clue to the treasure?'

'Of course it's a clue to the treasure!' he shouted. 'Think, girl! Think!'

'I'm trying,' I said. 'But sometimes if you try too hard you can't remember.' He was looming over me and his bushy eyebrows made him look very fierce. Out of the corner of my eye I saw our door-slave Caudex standing in the shadowed peristyle.

Probus must have seen Caudex, too, for he sat down again and used his handkerchief to mop his face. 'I'm sorry. I didn't mean to shout at you. Of course you need to think. I've had twenty years. You've only had a few moments. You know, I didn't think it was a clue at the time. I thought Virgil was repenting of something else. But later I began to wonder. I couldn't understand why he mentioned a flute, unless a silver flute was part of the hoard. I thought perhaps there were flute-like pipes in the house. But when I went back to check, the new owner told me there weren't any. The villa was beside the river, you see. Had no need of either pipes or well.'

'So you did go back.'

'Yes. About three years ago, shortly before I left Britannia. I was curious.'

'And there was a new owner?'

'Yes. The family living there were Britons. Relatives of Stephanos's wife. They had moved in to take care of the place until Stephanos and his family returned. But they never did.'

'So, they must have died,' I said. 'By the way, what happened to Boudica?'

'She and her army burned Londinium to the ground. Then they set off northwest and continued to burn and pillage. They burned a town called Verulamium where there were more Britons than Romans. Finally our troops caught up with her a few miles north of Verulamium. She took poison to avoid being humiliated in a Roman triumph.'

'Oh.'

'I spent the next fifteen years helping the governor rebuild Londinium. He made sure such Roman brutality never happened again. Then, after I was discharged and paid, I went to see the house one last time before I came home to Italia.'

I counted on my fingers. 'So you returned to that villa seventeen years after Stephanos hid his treasure there?'

'That's right. His wife's relatives were wary of me at first. Then I told them I had known Stephanos, which was true in a way. They warmed to me after that; ended up giving me dinner. They were building a wing onto one end of the house.'

'Maybe they found the treasure.'

'I don't think so. The building was going slowly. The father was barely scraping by with his wheat and barley crops, and a few chickens and sheep.'

'So,' I said. 'The house is still there, and presumably the treasure, too.'

'Yes.'

'And you have no idea at all where Virgil and Stephanos hid the treasure?'

'If I did, I wouldn't be here, would I?' he snapped. I must have looked surprised or hurt, for he quickly added, 'I'm sorry. What I mean to say is that I couldn't see anything resembling a flute or a pipe.'

'All right,' I said. 'Why don't we use the same method I used with Pandora? Let's close our eyes and travel there in our imagination. Can you remember the first time you saw it twenty years ago?'

'As if it was yesterday.'

'Can you describe it to me?' I opened my eyes a crack to make sure his were closed. They were.

'It was late March,' he said. 'Quite cold. Green hills, grey sky. A few buds on the bushes and trees.'

'Describe it in the present tense,' I said. 'As if it was happening right now.'

He sighed. 'Very well. Virgil and I arrive on horseback, expecting the worst. We ride along a dirt path. River on our left, thick trees either side of it, no houses in sight apart from this one-storey rustic villa with white walls, a slate roof and small arched windows. Fields over to the right, just beginning to show green, then hills. The owner must have heard our hoofbeats because he is waiting in the shelter of a little front porch as we ride up. It has just started to drizzle. When he sees we are soldiers, he looks very relieved. We dismount and each hitch our horse to a column.'

'Were the columns wood or marble?' I asked, wanting to have a clear picture in my head.

'Wood. Painted red for the bottom third and white for the top two thirds. There were two of them, holding up the little pitched roof before the entryway.'

'Good,' I said. 'Continue please.'

'The owner leads us inside, through double-doors, takes us to the kitchen and pours us some wine. As soon as we tell him about Boudica and her marauding army he grows pale. Says he had already decided to flee. His wife and sons are out back in the stables, loading their things on a cart. He agrees he should hide his treasure so it will be safe until he returns. That was when I went out back to help his family load the cart.'

'If he was rich he must have had slaves.'

Probus shook his head. 'Stephanos said his wife didn't approve. Most slaves in those days were Britons, of course, so it's understandable. She kept house and the two boys helped with the chickens and sheep and farm. Anyway, while I helped them pack, Virgil stayed in the villa with Stephanos to hide the treasure. About half an hour later, I brought the cart round with the wife and the two boys.'

'So Virgil and Stephanos had less than half an hour to hide the treasure.'

'Correct.'

I pointed at the roof tiles of our house. 'Could the word "flute" have referred to the curved clay tiles of a roof?' I asked.

'No. The house had flat tiles, made of slate or stone. Painted red, yellow and black.'

'What was the rest of the house made of. Do you remember?'

'The construction was flint on the lower walls then wattle and daub up above. A high pitched roof to let smoke from hearth and braziers disperse.'

'What's wattle and daub?'

'Wattle means woven wood. Daub is mud mixed with manure, straw and horse hair. You weave together the wood – hazel or willow – into something like a basket, only flat not curved. Fill it with wet daub and smooth some on either side. When it dries it makes a fairly good wall, especially if you plaster it with white lime. These wattle and daub walls are set onto sturdier flint walls usually about as high as my shoulder. In this house, I could see the bumpy part of the flint wall in the kitchen,' he added. 'It wasn't plastered as well as the other rooms.'

'So,' I said. 'To enter the house you pass through double doors. Then what?'

'You find yourself in a long corridor stretching left and right – all the length of the front of the house. It's lit by arched windows, four either side of the entryway. There are three doors leading off this corridor. The door to the kitchen and latrine on your left, the door to the reception dining room straight ahead, and the door to a bedroom complex on the right. The windows at the back of the house are square and have iron star grilles. They look out on the farmyard and stables and the fields beyond.'

'You went into all the rooms?'

'Yes. I went into the bedrooms to help them take out the last of their things. We took these along the corridor to the kitchen where a small back door led straight out into the farmyard. Vegetable patch, a few chicken coops and the stables.'

'How can you remember it so well?'

'Not one day has passed that I haven't thought about that villa. Gone over and over in my head where he might have hidden the treasure.'

'Could they have buried the treasure in one of the rooms of the house?'

'I don't think so. All the floors were either beaten chalk or mosaic. When I went back three years ago, I made sure I saw every room. All the floors looked undisturbed.'

'Was there a latrine hole?'

'Just the usual bucket in a little room near the kitchen. Also on a beaten chalk floor. And no hypocaust, as in some houses.'

'Tell me about the reception room?'

'It had a mosaic floor and frescoes on the walls and a little arched niche, too, which Stephanos used as his household shrine.'

'Eureka!' I cried. 'I've just remembered where I read that verse.'

'Where?' he cried, as excited as I was. 'Where is it from?'

'I think it's from Ovid,' I said, 'but Apollodorus mentions the same story.'

'What does it mean?'

'First tell me,' I said. 'Did any of the mosaics in the house have pictures of gods or goddesses or mythical creatures?'

His brow crinkled as he thought. 'No. They were all geometric designs.'

'Frescoes, then. You said there were frescoes on the walls?'

'Yes. In the reception room and bedrooms.'

'Pulchra, can you guess what I was thinking? Here's a clue. I next asked if the frescoes had any mythological scenes.'

'No,' he said. 'They were the old-fashioned kind. Coloured rectangles painted to look like marble below. Birds in large open panels up above.'

'No paintings of Athena or Apollo or satyrs, for example?'

'No. Not that I can remember.'

'Then I think I know where the hoard is hidden!'

'You do?'

'Tell me. When you brought the cart round to the front, were Virgil and Stephanos damp from being out in the drizzle, or dry from being inside?'

'Damp. And I remember their breath was steaming, like mine.'

'And their shoes? Any mud or dirt on them?'

Probus thoughtfully rubbed the callous beneath his chin. 'Virgil's caligae were muddy, like mine, because we'd been outside. But so were Stephanos's! What are you thinking?'

'I'm thinking that Virgil and Stephanos might have buried the hoard outside the house, not inside. After all, you were in the stables out back, you wouldn't have seen them if they buried the casket somewhere in front of the house.'

'Yes … YES! Now that you mention it, there was a spade leaning against the front of the house as we rode away. But if they buried the treasure outside the villa, it could be anywhere.'

'No, not anywhere. Now think. Among the trees beside the river, was there by any chance a pine tree? Or a single tree standing on its own?'

'A pine? Yes! There was one old pine tree a little distance from the other trees. I remember it stood out quite tall and stark against the grey sky.'

'Was it there when you went back three years ago?'

'Yes. I believe it was. But how did you know?'

'The verse your friend gasped with his dying breath refers to one of the Greek myths. Who in Greek mythology would repent over a flute? Or an aulos?'

'This is no time for childish riddles, girl! Tell me where the treasure is!'

'It's not a riddle. It's a clue to the whereabouts of the treasure. Virgil's last words: "I repent! I repent! A flute is not worth so great a price!" He was telling you where the treasure was buried. So I repeat: Who played a flute and then regretted it?'

'I don't know!'

'Marsyas, the satyr. Do you remember the story?'

'Remind me.'

'The goddess Athena invented the aulos, but when she blew on it her cheeks puffed out and the other goddesses mocked her. So she threw it away in disgust. Then the satyr Marsyas found it and he learned to play it so well that he decided to challenge Apollo to a contest.'

'Hubris,' said Probus.

'Yes. Marsyas lost the contest and as punishment for his overweening pride he was hung from a tree and Apollo skinned him alive.'

Probus shuddered and then frowned. 'But I still don't understand what that has to do with... Of course!'

'Yes. All the poets are in agreement. Marsyas was hung from a pine tree! Dig at the foot of the pine tree on the estate of Stephanos, and you will find your treasure.'

Probus leapt to his feet and nearly crushed my hand as he shook it. 'Thank you! Thank you!' he cried. 'I feel you are right. I shall sail for Britannia immediately.'

'Sir,' I said. 'If you do find the treasure, will you share it with the poor family who lives there now? After all, it really belongs to them.'

'Of course!' he said. 'Of course I'll share it!'

Whether I was right about the whereabouts of the treasure, only time will tell. I just hope that if he finds the treasure he shares it with that poor family. I have a feeling that he wasn't telling me everything.

So you see, dear Pulchra, how useful it is to know your myths, even the horrid ones?

Do you remember we promised to send each other a wise saying or an encouraging motto in our letters to one another? Just like Seneca? Here is one I have made up for you: Knowledge is the Greatest Treasure.

Cura ut valeas!

— AUTHOR'S NOTE —

Because this story takes place after *The Sirens of Surrentum*, in which Flavia and Pulchra promise to correspond, I thought I'd write it in the form of a letter. The description of the house with the treasure is based on the clever reconstruction of a Roman Villa at Butser Ancient Farm. If you are ever near Petersfield in Hampshire, you can visit the real thing.

DEATH BY
MEDUSA

**This story takes place on the Ides of August
AD 80 (between book XI, *The Sirens of Surrentum*
and book XII, *The Charioteer of Delphi*)**

On a beautiful summer morning in August a man dropped dead in front of Jonathan ben Mordecai.

Jonathan had been in lessons with his friends Flavia, Nubia and Lupus, but their tutor Aristo had a toothache, and had released them early.

There had been a summer storm the previous night, with a strong damp wind and lightning flashing out to sea. Now Lupus wrote something on his wax tablet and showed it to the others.

SOMETIMES STORMS WASH UP TREASURE FROM SHIPWRECKS he had written. LET'S GO TO BEACH

'Good idea, Lupus!' said Flavia. 'We'll take the dogs.'

Nubia nodded and so did Jonathan. He could look for seaweed. His father often added a spoonful of it – dried and pounded – to his concoctions.

The beach was deserted. It was too late in the day for the fishermen, who had already brought in their catch, and it was too early for the townspeople, who were still at work or in lessons. The previous night's storm had cleared the air, so that the lofty bowl of the sky was a flawless blue. There was no breath of wind. From the lighthouse of Portus, five miles north, the plume of smoke rose as straight as a dark thread on a plumb line.

Jonathan took a deep, grateful breath. The air was

so pure and clear that he could fill his asthmatic lungs right up to the top. It felt good. As he and his friends topped a dune, the dogs raced down to the water.

Suddenly the dogs stopped and began to bark as a man rose out of the sea about twenty feet in front of them. He was thin and grizzled and naked apart from a small loincloth. He staggered out of the surf and across the sand, his arms stretched out towards them, his eyes bulging. There was a look of such pure horror on his face that Jonathan uttered an oath in Hebrew. Flavia and Nubia both screamed, and Lupus gave a grunt of surprise.

Abruptly the man threw open his arms, uttered an incoherent cry and fell back onto the sand, only a few feet away from them. As the man lay twitching, Flavia and Nubia screamed again, but Jonathan rushed forward. His father was a doctor and his natural instinct was to give medical aid.

'Are you all right?' asked Jonathan, kneeling beside the man. 'What's wrong?'

'I'm dying!' gasped the man. 'Dying!'

'How?' asked Jonathan. 'Who?' He was aware of Flavia and Lupus coming to stand either side of him and of Nubia holding back the dogs.

The man fixed his terrible gaze on each of the children in turn. 'Medusa!' he gasped. 'Get vinegar!' For a few terrible moments his mouth opened and closed, like a fish on dry land. Then he gave the death rattle and his bulging eyes set in an unseeing stare.

'He's dead.' Jonathan's heart was pounding and he felt his lungs tightening, so that he had to fight for air. 'I couldn't help him,' he wheezed. 'I don't know what's wrong with him.'

'Oh, no!' cried Flavia. 'Who is he? Where did he come from?'

'I don't know.' Jonathan groped for the herb pouch around his neck and pressed it to his nose. 'Nubia, get the dogs away from him.'

Nubia pulled the dogs back and bent to attach their leashes to their collars.

Still breathing from his herb pouch, Jonathan stood up and gazed down at the dead man's face, swollen and frozen in a mask of horror. Jonathan's lungs were loosening a little but his heart was still pounding hard.

'Medusa,' whispered Nubia, 'is mythical monster with snakes for hair. She is being so ugly she turns those who see her to stone.'

'Yes,' murmured Flavia. 'And he looks exactly like someone killed by looking at Medusa.'

'Impossible,' wheezed Jonathan. 'Medusa is . . . a mythical monster. She doesn't . . . really exist.'

'Are we sure of that?' said Flavia, making the sign against evil.

Lupus grunted and pointed at some marks on the man's shoulder. Jonathan let go of his herb pouch, bent down and gingerly rolled the body over onto its side. The girls gasped. Beneath a coating of sand, the man's bony back was crisscrossed by red weals.

'Great Juno's beard!' wheezed Jonathan. 'Someone … has given him … a terrible beating.'

'Maybe he is slave,' suggested Nubia. 'And his master is whipping him.'

'No,' said Flavia. 'Look at his right hand. He's wearing a gold signet ring. Those are usually only worn by Roman citizens of the equestrian class, like my father. Can you make out what's on the intaglio, Jonathan? I can't bear to touch him.'

Jonathan bent to examine the man's finger. 'This one is made … of dark blue glass,' he said. 'It shows a goddess. Maybe one of the Muses. And the ring isn't gold; I think it's copper. His finger is green underneath.' Jonathan's heart was still pounding but his breathing was easier.

'Behold!' said Nubia. 'Dark stains on fingers of his left hand.'

'I wonder what that could be?' said Flavia.

Jonathan shook his head. A few paces away, on the other side of a low dune, Lupus gave an inarticulate cry of triumph and held up a man's tunic.

'Lupus has found his clothes!' said Flavia.

Jonathan followed the girls and the three dogs over

a sand dune to Lupus. The dogs excitedly sniffed a pair of sandals and a leather belt-pouch in the sand.

Flavia took the tunic from Lupus and held it up. It was unbleached linen and in places the material was so thin that Jonathan could see sunlight shining through. He could also see where it had been mended.

'It's very old and threadbare,' Flavia murmured. 'He can't have been very rich. And it doesn't have the stripes of a patrician or equestrian, so he's probably a plebeian.' Flavia handed the tunic back to Lupus, who looked at it, shrugged and then dropped it on the sand.

Jonathan picked up the sandals. 'These sandals are ancient, too. This one's been repaired with twine.'

'May I see?' asked Flavia. Jonathan handed them over. 'The metal studs on the bottom make an 'S' shape,' she said. 'The studs that are left, that is.'

'Behold!' said Nubia, pulling Tigris back by his collar. 'Naked footprints leading down to sea. He undresses and walks into water.'

'Or maybe,' said Flavia, 'he ran into the water, pursued by his enemy!'

'No,' said Nubia. 'Behold, footprints are light and not so far apart. If person or animal runs on sand, they leave deep footprints and farther apart.' She pointed to their own footprints.

'Of course!' said Flavia. 'If you run, then you land

harder and each stride is longer than usual. How did you know that, Nubia?'

'My family was keeping goats. I often was having to track lost ones.'

'If he was walking,' said Jonathan, 'then he can't have been worried. He was just strolling down to the sea.'

Lupus was examining the man's belt pouch. Jonathan watched him spread the tunic on the sand and empty the contents of the pouch onto it: one sestertius and three quadrans, a chewed piece of mastic gum, a wooden stylus and some lint. Something else was filling the pouch. Something flat and square. Lupus gave the pouch a shake and out fell a small wax tablet. As Lupus read it, his eyebrows went up. He stood up and held it out for them to see.

Before Jonathan could read the words written on it, Flavia had snatched it from Lupus.

'It's just a list of errands,' she said, and then gasped.

'What is it?' asked Jonathan, coming to read over her shoulder.

Flavia pointed: *'Pick up toga from fullers', see Rufus and Dexter, new collar for Garum, kill Artotrogus!'* She looked up at him, wide-eyed. 'He's written "kill Artotrogus" on his list of things to do!'

'Arty togas?' asked Nubia with a frown.

'Not arty togas,' said Flavia, 'Artotrogus. It's a Greek name which means "bread eater". I'm sure I've heard it before ...' She thoughtfully sucked a loose strand of light brown hair.

'Maybe the person named Artotrogus killed *him*,' said Jonathan, looking at the dead man, 'before he could kill Artotrogus.'

'Then Artotrogus might still be here!' cried Flavia.

Jonathan shaded his eyes and quickly looked around.

To the north he could see the synagogue, then the warehouses and docks of the Marina Harbour. To the east were dunes and a few tombs of the dead. To the south was a long stretch of undulating beach, flanked by a grove of umbrella pines and oak trees. And to the west was the blue Tyrrhenian Sea. But there was nobody in sight on either land or sea.

'Lupus,' said Flavia. 'Could you search the beach to the south, towards Laurentum? Look for footprints with a broken "S" shape on the sole. And Jonathan, can you search the other way? Towards town? Even if we can't catch the culprit, maybe we can find his footprints and see which direction he came from. And maybe we can find the place where he and his killer struggled.'

'Why don't you and Nubia search the beach to the north?' said Jonathan. 'I want to examine the body more closely. Unless you'd rather do that.'

Flavia glanced over at the corpse. 'No,' she said with a shudder. 'Nubia and I will go north. Nubia, can you go on to the Marina Harbour and alert the vigiles? And take the dogs with you so they don't trample evidence?'

As the two girls and the dogs set off towards Ostia and as Lupus hurried away in the opposite direction, Jonathan took a deep breath and turned back to the body.

He squatted on his haunches and tried to study the victim without feeling sick. The man was perhaps thirty-five years old. He was very thin, which made his swollen face look strange. His arms and legs were fairly brown, but not as tanned as a labourer's.

The whip had been wielded with such force that some of the weals curved round the dead man's shoulders and ribs. There were also several stripes on the front of his right thigh, as if he had faced his attacker for a moment. Finally, Jonathan forced himself to look at the man's contorted face. He was clean-shaven but had not been to the barber in at least two days. His face was blotched and swollen. His lips were blue and Jonathan could just make out the tip of his tongue protruding.

Jonathan frowned. Something didn't make sense. The man's face suggested he had been a victim of poisoning. But his body showed he had been brutally whipped.

Jonathan stood up and gazed thoughtfully out to sea for a few moments. He and his friends had spent the previous month studying poisons in Surrentum, in order to prevent a killing. In the course of their investigations they had met the daughter of Nero's infamous poisoner, Locusta. Upon their return they had come across a case of poisoning right here in Ostia. Could this really be another case? Or did he just have poison too much in the front of his mind?

Jonathan shaded his eyes and looked south-east, in the direction Lupus had gone. Lupus was wandering back and forth on the sand, head down, looking for footprints. He saw Jonathan watching and gave a shrug as if to say: Still no luck.

Jonathan nodded and turned to the north. Flavia had obviously found something. She was crouching down and examining the sand.

He went to her, and as his shadow fell across her, she looked up.

'What is it?' he asked.

'Footprints of sandals with the broken "S" on the soles.' She stood up and pointed. 'See? There's a line of them. Walking not running.' They both looked in the direction the footprints had come. In the distance Jonathan could see Nubia and the dogs; they had reached the docks.

'He came from town,' said Flavia, 'walked along the beach, took off his tunic and sandals and left them over there in a neat pile, then went down to the water.

'Maybe he went to bathe his wounds in the sea,' asked Jonathan. 'If you have open wounds, salt water hurts like Hades but it speeds up the healing.'

'So you think someone flogged him in town, and that afterwards he got dressed, came here, took off his clothes and went to bathe his wounds? Then why isn't there blood on his tunic?'

'Maybe they flogged him here, after he got undressed.'

'But there are no other footprints. He came alone and went into the sea alone, too.'

'Could the killer have come from the sea?' mused Jonathan. 'And then gone back out that way? There's a fishing boat out there.'

'But that boat wasn't here earlier,' said Flavia. 'And those three ships on the horizon are too far away. There's no wind,' she added, 'so a boatman would have to row very hard.'

'And nobody could row away that fast,' said Jonathan with a sigh. 'We would have seen him.'

'You don't think Medusa really appeared to him, do you?'

'No,' said Jonathan.

'Then why did he say "Medusa"?'

'Maybe a very ugly woman killed him?' said Jonathan. 'Maybe the hideously ugly wife of Artotrogus?'

Flavia gave a queasy smile and handed him the wax tablet. 'Look at this.' She pointed at the dead man's list.

'Rufus and Dexter are bankers,' said Jonathan. 'Maybe he was going to make a withdrawal.'

'Or take out a loan,' said Flavia. 'That's their specialty. But I wasn't pointing at them. I was pointing at this: one of his errands was to get a new collar for Garum. Garum is obviously the name of a dog.'

'Or a slave,' said Jonathan.

'He doesn't look rich enough to own a slave. But if he has a dog named Garum then maybe he named his other dog Vinegar. That could explain why he said "Get Vinegar"!'

Jonathan raised an eyebrow. 'A dog called Vinegar? I doubt it.'

Flavia shrugged. 'Well, he named one pet after a condiment— Look. Here comes Lupus. He obviously hasn't found anything.'

'But Nubia has,' said Jonathan, and pointed with his chin. 'It seems she's found someone to help us. Our old friend Marcus Artorius Bato.'

Bato was a short man with thinning hair and pale eyes, not yet thirty. He had helped the friends with their first mystery and he had also sailed with them to Rhodes in search of a criminal mastermind. Jonathan knew that although Bato was not officially a magistrate this year, he was an ambitious man, and that he was already thinking ahead to next year's elections. He often loitered outside the magistrate's offices, so that if they were too busy he himself could offer assistance to the citizens of Ostia.

Bato gave them a cool smile. 'Salve, Flavia Gemina,' he said. 'Salvete, Jonathan and Lupus. Your friend Nubia saw me coming out of the harbourmaster's office. She told me you witnessed a man's death. I've sent for the vigiles. Where is the body?'

'Over there,' said Jonathan.

Bato followed them over to the naked body in the sand. The man still lay on his side, as Jonathan had left him.

'By Hercules,' muttered Bato. 'Flogged to death. That's not a pretty sight.' He made the sign against evil.

'Actually,' said Jonathan. 'I don't think the flogging killed him. I think he died of poisoning.'

'What?' said Flavia and Bato together.

'Look at his face. It's swollen and blotchy. His tongue is swollen, too, and his lips are blue. And one of his dying words was "vinegar".'

'Vinegar?' said Bato. 'And that makes you suspect poison?'

Jonathan nodded. 'Vinegar is often used as an antidote to poison.'

'Either that,' said Flavia, 'or Vinegar is the name of a dog.'

Bato raised both eyebrows at her, then turned back to Jonathan. 'How is vinegar an antidote?'

'It induces vomiting. My father has twice used vinegar as an antidote to belladonna and once for mandrake.'

'A few weeks ago,' said Flavia, 'Jonathan used vinegar to save the life of a little boy.'

'But wouldn't drinking salt-water have the same effect?' said Bato. 'And there is plenty of that here.'

'True,' said Jonathan, and frowned.

'Doctor Mordecai is sometimes bathing wounds in vinegar,' offered Nubia. 'Perhaps he wanted vinegar for cuts from whip.'

'That flogging must have been painful,' said Jonathan, 'but it wasn't what killed him. Something else did. And he knew he was dying. He told us he was dying. I think he needed vinegar as an antidote.'

'Well, it's too late for an antidote now,' said Bato, and mopped his forehead with a handkerchief. 'Did he say anything else before he died?'

'Yes,' said Jonathan. 'He cried out the name "Medusa".'

Bato looked up sharply. 'Are you sure?'

Jonathan shrugged. 'His voice was very hoarse. I might have misunderstood.'

'You didn't misunderstand,' said Flavia. 'We heard it, too.'

Bato shook his head in wonder.

'Medusa,' said Nubia, 'is hideous monster who turns those who see her to stone.'

'I know that,' snapped Bato. 'Everyone knows that. But she's not real. She couldn't have killed him. Do you know who the victim is?' he added.

'No,' said Flavia. 'He died before he could tell us.'

'The only mark of identification is his signet ring,' said Jonathan. 'I think it shows one of the Muses.'

Bato knelt in the sand and lifted the man's limp right hand. 'She's holding a little mask. Could be Melpomene,' he muttered. 'Or Thalia. But I've never seen its imprint on a document, and therefore I don't know the owner.' He stood up and brushed the sand from his knees.

'There was nothing else to identify him,' said Flavia, 'but we did find his list of things to do.' She handed over the wax tablet.

Bato's eyes opened in surprise as he read the last entry, then he snorted.

'Artotrogus. The Parasite.'

'You know Artotrogus?' said Jonathan.

'I don't know a real Artotrogus,' said Bato. 'It's the name of the Parasite in the comedies of Plautus. One of his stock characters.'

'Of course!' said Flavia. 'That's where I've heard the name.'

'What is parasite?' asked Nubia with a frown. 'Is it not animal that lives on another animal? Like lice or leeches?'

'Yes,' said Bato, 'but it can also mean the sort of man who lives off others. You know the type. Always coming round at dinner time and then inviting himself to stay and eat.'

'He's a comical character in Roman comedy,' added Flavia. 'He's often shown with a huge napkin which he fills with food from the dinner party.'

'So there's no real Artotrogus in Ostia?' asked Jonathan.

'I've not come across anyone by that name,' said Bato. 'And I've spent the last two years knee deep in town records.'

Lupus grunted and pointed in the direction of the town.

Flavia and the others turned to see two vigiles jogging towards them across the sand. They had a stretcher between them.

Bato looked at Jonathan. 'Your father is a doctor, isn't he?'

'Yes.'

'A good one?'

'The best. He studied medicine in Alexandria.'

The vigiles came to a panting halt before the

group and looked down at the body.

'Remind me of your father's full name and where you live?' continued Bato, without looking at the vigiles.

'His name is Mordecai ben Ezra,' replied Jonathan. 'We live on Green Fountain Street.'

Bato turned to the vigiles. 'Take the body to Doctor Mordecai ben Ezra on Green Fountain Street. See if he can determine the cause of death. Then take him to the barracks until we can identify him.'

'I can identify him,' said one of the vigiles, a sandy-haired soldier with a sprinkling of freckles across his face. 'It's Valens, the poet.'

'Poet?' said Bato.

'Yeah,' said Freckles. 'Didn't recognise him at first because his face is all swollen up. But that's him. He writes comedies. Put one on for the last Floralia. It wasn't bad. My brother's a carpenter. Helps build the sets sometimes.'

'Of course!' cried Flavia. 'I should have guessed he was a writer or a scholar. His fingers are stained with ink and bear the writer's callous. But because the stains are on his left hand rather than his right, I didn't think of that.'

'Then he's left-handed,' said Jonathan.

'Yes,' said Flavia. 'Silly me.'

'Do you know where Valens lives?' Bato asked

Freckles, and then corrected himself. 'Used to live?'

'No idea. My brother would, though. His name's Gaius Vettius Silvanus. Lives on Ropemaker's Street near the Roman Gate. Has a little workshop there with a room above. He'll tell you where Valens lives.'

Gaius Vettius Silvanus put down his adze and looked up.

'Valens? Dead? Poor wretch.'

'What can you tell us about him?' said Bato.

Jonathan and his friends were standing behind Bato in the hot, dim workshop. The dogs were eagerly sniffing furniture. Scuto sneezed. The smell of pine pitch and sawdust made Jonathan want to sneeze, too.

Silvanus picked up a rag and mopped his freckled brow. 'I can tell you he lived above a tavern near here—'

'Eureka!' cried Flavia, and looked at her friends. 'Medusa! Was it the Medusa Tavern?'

'Yes,' said Jonathan. 'That might explain his last words!'

'No,' said Silvanus. 'It was Perpetua's place over by the Baths of Claudius. Just around the corner from here.'

'Oh,' said Flavia, and gave Jonathan a disappointed shrug.

'Did Valens have any enemies?' asked Bato.

'Anyone who would want him dead?'

'Well there was that man his dog bit. Happened a few days ago. Man took him to court.'

'Eureka!' cried Flavia. 'Was the man's name Artotrogus?'

Silvanus shook his head. 'Man's name was Sutor. A cobbler. Poor Valens had to pay a fine and promise not to take the dog out again unless he was on a proper lead.'

'Eureka!' cried Flavia a third time. 'Was the dog's name Garum?'

Jonathan rolled his eyes, but to his surprise Silvanus nodded. 'As a matter of fact, I think it was.'

Sutor the cobbler had a tiny workshop only a few doors down from Silvanus. It was almost noon and he was just putting away his tools when the four friends, their three dogs and Marcus Artorius Bato came to his shop front. A counter separated the workshop in back from the waiting area at the front. This waiting area contained a battered rattan chair and a three legged stool. Jonathan supposed Sutor sat on it to measure people's feet.

'Get those dogs away from here!' yelled Sutor. He was a middle-aged man with a mop of dark hair and a single eyebrow. 'Far away!'

Nubia nodded and pulled the three dogs back through the doorway and out of sight.

'Something tells me you lot aren't here for shoes,' grumbled the cobbler when she had gone.

'We're investigating a suspicious death,' said Bato in his most official voice. 'Man named Valens. We understand you took him to court last week.'

'That I did.' Sutor raised a wooden flap in the counter and came into the waiting area. He showed them an ugly bite mark on his left calf. 'Look where his dog bit me.'

'Ouch!' said Jonathan. Lupus grunted his agreement.

'What was the judge's verdict?' asked Bato.

'Valens had to pay me a fine. It was barely enough to cover the doctor's fee. And the judge ordered him to buy a proper collar and leash for the dog. It was only on a piece of twine.'

'Where were you this morning,' asked Flavia. 'About an hour ago?'

Sutor stared at Bato. 'Who's this. Your daughter?'

Jonathan and Lupus exchanged an amused glance.

'Just answer the question,' snapped Bato. 'Valens dropped dead at their feet just under an hour ago.'

'Well, I've been here all morning, haven't I? You can ask anyone in the neighbourhood.'

'We will,' said Bato. 'Thank you for your cooperation.'

'Wait,' said Flavia. 'Do you happen to have a

customer called Artotrogus? Or know anyone of that name?'

'No. I don't.'

Lupus had been examining the half-made shoes on the counter. Now he picked up a sole of a shoe and showed it to the others.

'You put a hobnail 'S' on the bottom of your shoes?' said Jonathan.

'Yeah, I do. I put it on all my outdoor shoes. Stands for Sutor. It's my special mark.'

'So Valens had bought shoes from you before?' asked Flavia.

'Yes. Came in for a new pair last week. But his dog bit me before he could pay. Was trying to get me to come down on the price. I suppose he didn't make much money writing plays. If you want a steady income, be a cobbler, not a writer.'

'Thanks,' said Bato drily. 'We'll remember that.'

Outside Perpetua's Tavern, Bato turned to them. 'I can't have the four of you and your dogs trailing around after me all day.'

'All right,' said Flavia. 'Nubia, can you and Lupus take the dogs home? And find out what Jonathan's father thinks the cause of death was? Jonathan and I will go with Bato. We'll meet you back at Jonathan's house in half an hour.'

Lupus and Nubia nodded and followed the

straining dogs down Ropemaker's Street in the direction of home.

Flavia and Jonathan turned back to Bato. 'Better?' said Flavia.

Bato sighed. 'I suppose. Come on.'

He led the way into the tavern. It was a cool, dim space with sawdust on the floor and half a dozen wooden trestle tables. Several men were sitting and eating sausages and soup. It smelt of musty wine and frying sausage. A door at the far end of the room led to a sunny, green inner courtyard.

'Three for lunch?' said a woman, coming out from behind the bar. She was cheerful and plump, with dark frizzy hair and a faint moustache on her upper lip. Jonathan guessed she was about thirty years old.

'I'm Marcus Artorius Bato,' said Bato. 'We're investigating the death of a man called Valens. Did you know him?'

'Quintus? Dead?' gasped the woman. Her face went pale. 'I don't believe it. He was here this morning. Seemed fine to me.'

'He showed no signs of being poisoned?' asked Jonathan.

'Shhh!' hissed Perpetua, as some of the diners looked up from their soup in alarm. 'Let's discuss this in private.' She clapped her hands to get the attention of a girl behind the counter. 'Felicia!' she cried. 'Take over here. I must talk to these people.

Bring some wine to the triclinium. Some of the Surrentinum.' And to Bato: 'There's a private dining-room at the back. I sometimes hire it out but it's empty today.'

She led them past the bar, out the door, through the shaded inner courtyard – where more men were eating and drinking – and into a small triclinium with red-and-mustard coloured panels on the walls.

'Tell us about Valens,' said Bato, sitting on one of the couches.

'I need a drink first,' said Perpetua as Felicia brought in a tray with two jugs, four beakers, and a plate of olives. 'Half and half?' she said to Bato.

'Please. And well-watered for the children.'

Perpetua mixed their wine. Jonathan drank his gratefully. It was very weak and slightly vinegary but cold and refreshing. 'Your children?' asked Perpetua, looking from Jonathan to Flavia and back.

Bato gave a half-smile. 'My assistants,' he said, and his face grew serious. 'They saw Valens die.'

'Tell me!' cried Perpetua, taking a gulp of wine. 'What happened?'

'First tell us about Valens,' said Bato.

'Well, he lives upstairs. Has done for five or six years. Always pays his rent on time, though sometimes I wonder how he does it. He's a good tenant. And his dog Garum is a good watchdog. I let him sleep in the tavern at night and we never have any robberies. That's Garum you hear barking now. Doesn't like being cooped up, but he bit someone last week and Gaius went off to buy a collar and lead.'

'Does he also have a dog called Vinegar?' asked Flavia.

'Why no, bless you. Why would he have a dog called Vinegar?'

'Well, if he has a dog called Garum…'

'That's because ever since he was a puppy, Garum has loved fish-sauce. Goes mad for it.'

'But he doesn't like vinegar?'

'Not that I know of.' She frowned at Bato. 'What does this have to do with his death?'

'Nothing,' said Bato drily. 'What else can you tell us? What was his full name? Does he have any friends or family? What did he do before he came here?'

Perpetua poured herself another beaker of wine and took a sip. 'His full name is Quintus Hostilius Valens. No family I know of. He used to be a sailor but had to give up after a nasty experience. He fell overboard once, off some Greek island.'

'And he couldn't swim?' asked Bato.

'Oh, he could swim all right. He does thirty laps in the pool at the baths every day, when he can afford to go. But when he was a sailor he got stung by a mass of jellyfish and they nearly killed him. Doctor told him if it happened again, he'd die. So he gave up being a sailor and became a poet.'

'Great Juno's beard!' exclaimed Jonathan. 'I know how he died!'

Flavia looked at him in astonishment.

'You do?' said Bato, a tinge of envy in his voice.

Jonathan nodded and looked at Flavia. 'Remember the sea near Cyrene on our trip to Rhodes?' he said. 'After that bad storm?'

'Of course!' she cried. 'Jonathan you're brilliant! Those whip marks weren't whip marks, were they?'

'No,' said Jonathan. 'They were something completely different. And they *were* the cause of death.'

'What are you two talking about?' said Bato, clearly annoyed.

Flavia ignored him and turned to Perpetua. 'Just answer one question. Was Artotrogus a character in a play he was writing?'

'Why, yes! How did you know that?'

'Just a lucky guess.' Flavia turned to Lupus and Bato. 'Come on,' she said. 'Let's go see whether Doctor Mordecai agrees with Jonathan's deduction.'

'Wait!' cried Perpetua. 'You didn't tell me how he died!'

'He went for a swim in the sea,' said Flavia. 'Probably because he couldn't afford the baths.'

'And?' said Perpetua.

'And,' said Jonathan, 'a jellyfish stung him to death.'

'You were right in your deduction, my son.' Jonathan's father pulled a sheet over Valens's body. He and Bato and the four friends were standing in Jonathan's cool atrium, where the body was laid out on a marble bench. 'The marks left by a jellyfish's tendrils do resemble those of a studded whip. This sting will cause most people acute discomfort for a time, but rarely death. However, certain people have a very bad reaction; they are particularly susceptible. I heard of several cases when I was studying in Alexandria; the patient's throat swells and he is unable to breathe. He dies of suffocation.' He put his hand on Jonathan's shoulder. 'It's not unlike a very bad asthma attack. This poor man was obviously one of the susceptible ones. If, as you say, he was badly stung as a young man then that could make the reaction to a subsequent attack even worse. The doctor told him – rightly – that if he was ever stung again it could kill him.'

'Why did he go swimming, if he knew the danger?' asked Flavia.

'I doubt he suspected any danger,' said Mordecai. 'I have never seen such a jellyfish here in Ostia. Last night's storm must have blown some in. He was just unlucky. Very unlucky.'

'Why did he ask for vinegar?' said Bato

'Vinegar is the one thing that can counteract the sting of a jellyfish. Water will make it worse, as will urine or any of the other usual remedies. His doctor must have told him this.'

Flavia looked at Nubia. 'You were right! He wanted vinegar to bathe his wounds.'

'Well done,' said Mordecai to Nubia. Then he turned to Jonathan. 'But even if you had been carrying vinegar on you, I don't think you could have saved him.'

Jonathan nodded and stared at the floor. He wondered if his father just said that to be kind.

'Why was he saying name of Medusa?' asked Nubia.

'Don't you remember?' said Flavia. 'I told you once before. Some people call jellyfish a medusa. Because the tentacles look like Medusa's snaky hair.'

'Oh yes,' said Nubia and she looked at the body under its sheet. 'Poor man.'

'Yes,' agreed Jonathan. 'What a horrible way to go. Death by Medusa.'

— AUTHOR'S NOTE —

This story was inspired by a depiction of Sherlock Holmes at Baker Street tube station, near where the fictional detective 'lived'. The picture – on tiles of the Bakerloo line – shows Holmes at the seaside, finding a man dying in agony on the beach. The man's last words are 'The lion's mane!' Intrigued by this, I looked up the story, which is called 'The Lion's Mane.' I love the idea that someone's last words can be so mysterious and exciting. In the Sherlock Holmes mystery story there is a long investigation, with lots of 'red herrings'. It finally turns out that the 'Lion's Mane' is a type of jellyfish, and that the man's death was an unhappy accident.

In Roman times – and even today – people sometimes call jellyfish 'medusa'. So I had the idea for my story right there.

THE PERSEUS
PROPHECY

This story takes place on the last day of October
AD 80 between book XII, *The Charioteer from
Delphi* and book XIII, *The Slave Girl of Jerusalem*

Flavia Gemina and Jonathan ben Mordecai were playing a game of latrunculi at Jonathan's house when they heard a pounding on the front door.

'Must be Lupus and Nubia.' Jonathan put down his black pebble marker and stood up. 'Back early from walking the dogs.'

'But they went out the back door,' said Flavia. 'That pounding is coming from your front door.'

'Doctor! Help! Come quickly!' A man's voice from the street, muffled by the door.

Flavia followed Jonathan out of the tablinum and through the atrium to the vestibule. Jonathan unbolted the front door and pulled it open. A young man stood there, breathing hard. The blustery autumn wind pasted his short pine-green tunic against his muscular body. He was very handsome with smooth tanned skin and glossy black hair, and his long-lashed brown eyes were wide with panic.

'Where's the doctor?' cried the man, looking past them. 'My wife's had an accident!'

'My father's out,' said Jonathan. 'But I can help. I often assist him.'

'All right.' The man had a slight Greek accent. 'Come quickly. We're just up the street.'

Flavia and Jonathan turned right out of the front door and followed the man up Green Fountain Street towards the Roman Gate. Flavia pulled her sky-blue palla tighter around her shoulders; the wind was making the last dry leaves of the mulberry trees skitter along the pavement. A dozen houses from Jonathan's, a door stood open.

'In here,' cried the man. 'In here!'

The two friends followed him through the atrium. Like many of the houses on Green Fountain Street, this one had an inner garden with a columned peristyle around it. At the far end of the garden, Flavia saw a woman in a pink stola and lavender cloak lying on her back. Her head lay between two columns of the peristyle and her body was spread-eagled on one of the pebbled paths of the garden.

As Flavia came nearer, she saw that the woman was middle-aged, with a heavily-powdered, pockmarked face. Her elaborate wig was slightly askew and her eyes were fixed and staring; she was clearly dead. Flavia shuddered and looked away.

Jonathan knelt on the mosaic walkway beside the woman, and pressed the fingers of his right hand to her neck. Flavia forced herself to look back.

Now she saw the bloody dent just above the woman's left eyebrow and the blood pooling beneath her wig and soaking the lavender hood of her cloak. Near the woman's head lay a marble disc, about the size of a dinner plate. It bore a painted relief of the Greek hero Perseus holding the head of

Medusa. A short leather thong was attached to a hole drilled near the top of the marble disc, and its bottom edge was bloody.

Flavia looked around the garden. Between each pair of columns hung similar discs. She had seen them before, at her uncle's townhouse in Rome. She knew they were called oscilla and that they were supposed to frighten away birds and evil spirits. The gusting wind was making them revolve and she realised that each was painted with a hero from Greek mythology. There was no oscillum above the woman's head, just a dangling leather thong, moving slightly in the strong breeze.

Jonathan closed the woman's eyes, shook his head and stood up. 'I'm afraid there's nothing I can do. She's dead.'

'Poor Priscilla,' said the man. 'I was upstairs, but it's obvious what happened. She was standing here when the oscillum fell and hit her.'

'What are the odds,' murmured Jonathan, 'that she would be standing right underneath it when it fell?'

The man shrugged. 'The wind must have blown it down.'

Flavia moved between two of the columns and squatted down to study the oscillum. She fingered the severed thong. 'Who else was in the house?' she asked sharply.

'Nobody,' said the man. 'All our slaves have gone ahead to Rome. My wife– We have a town-house there.'

'Were the front and back doors closed and bolted?'

'Yes. I think so.'

'Did you move the body?' asked Flavia.

'No. I didn't even touch her.' He looked at Jonathan. 'I wanted your father to write a certificate of death for her,' he said. 'Can you do it instead?'

Jonathan frowned. 'I suppose I could write—'

'No, Jonathan!' interrupted Flavia. 'Don't you remember? You have to do it in the presence of a magistrate.' She raised her eyebrows at him.

'Do I?' said Jonathan. 'Oh. Yes. Um. Who do we—'

'Sir,' said Flavia to the man. 'Can you go and get one of the magistrates from the forum? We'll wait here with the body.'

'Are you sure that's necessary?'

'Yes,' said Flavia, and lied: 'When my mother tragically died in childbirth last year, we had to get the magistrates to confirm the cause of death was natural.'

'Very well,' said the man. 'I'll be back within the hour.'

'Sir!' cried Flavia, as the man turned to go. 'What's your name?'

'My name is Titus Flavius Perseus. My wife was called Priscilla. Sulpicia Priscilla.' He gave her body a lingering look, then turned and hurried out of the garden.

'Jonathan!' hissed Flavia, after Perseus had gone. 'Something's not right here. That's why I sent him to find the magistrate. So we can accuse him in front of someone official.'

'Accuse him?'

'Look,' said Flavia. 'The wound on her head is on her eyebrow. Look at the angle. The only way she could have got such a wound is if she were looking up at the oscillum at the very moment it fell. Think about it! The wound should be on the top of her head!'

Jonathan nodded. 'And her wig would have cushioned the blow,' he said.

'Even if she *was* looking up,' said Flavia. 'The position of her body is wrong. Her feet are in the garden. If she had been standing under the oscillum her feet would be between the pillars and her head would be in the garden. Or on the walkway.'

'Great Jupiter's eyebrows!' muttered Jonathan. 'It's as if someone placed her there, with her head below the oscillum.'

'Exactly,' said Flavia. 'And look here: this thong has been cut! It didn't break. I believe someone cut the oscillum down, hit her on the head, then placed the disc and the body so that it would look like an accident.'

The wind moaned and made the garden shrubs tremble.

'Great Juno's beard,' muttered Jonathan. 'I think you're right.'

Flavia stood up and pulled her palla around her shoulders. She walked slowly along the sheltered walkway towards the atrium, looking left and right.

Jonathan followed. 'What are we looking for?'

'Motive,' said Flavia, and as they reached the atrium she cried. 'Ecce!' She ran past the impluvium and bent to open a leather satchel in the vestibule beside the door.

'What is it?'

Flavia pulled out a fistful of gold jewelry. 'Evidence that she was about to divorce him and take her dowry back home with her.'

'How is that evidence?'

'There's only one bag here,' said Flavia, digging deep. 'Full of women's clothing and jewelry. They weren't going back to Rome together. She was going alone. Did you notice her name? Sulpicia Priscilla?'

'So?'

'Highborn. Patrician. From a good rich family.'

'And his name, Titus Flavius Perseus,' said Jonathan, 'shows he's a freedman. He probably used to be an imperial slave.'

Flavia nodded. 'Exactly. He was handsome and young, but still an ex-slave. Priscilla married beneath her. Maybe she began to have second thoughts.'

Jonathan looked towards the body in the garden. 'He certainly didn't marry her for her looks.'

Flavia held up a blue silk palla shot with gold thread. 'He probably married her for her money. Even if he wasn't named in her will, he could have sold some of her clothing and jewelry and made a fortune.'

'Poor Priscilla,' said Jonathan.

Flavia nodded sadly. 'In Greek mythology,' she said, 'it was prophesied that the hero Perseus would kill his grandfather Acrisius. And he did, with a discus. But that was an accident. The Perseus who lives here killed his wife with a kind of discus, too. But it was no accident. It was murder.'

— AUTHOR'S NOTE —

The first time I saw an oscillum in a museum, I couldn't imagine what it was. A decorated discus? A strange type of wall decoration? A bumpy plate? Then, when I visited the site of Herculaneum in the shadow of Vesuvius, I saw how the Romans used to hang these discs between the pillars of a peristyle. Presumably they were used for decoration but perhaps also to avert evil and/or scare away birds. I wrote this in my writer's notebook:

Idea: A marble oscillum has apparently fallen and crushed the skull of a rich man or woman. At first it looks like an accident, but Flavia wonders . . . Killer waits for a blustery autumn wind, rattling the shutters, slamming doors, twirling oscilla, and exciting the wind chimes. Drugs the woman, then cuts the oscillum and strikes her head with it, leaves it near the body beneath where it hung.

THE FIVE
BARLEY GRAINS

This story takes place three days after the
Ides of November AD 80 (before the events of
Roman Mystery XIII, *The Slave Girl from Jerusalem*)

It was a dark and stormy night in the Roman port of Ostia, and Flavia Gemina was in a bad mood.

'Oh, Pollux!' she cursed, as she pricked her thumb with a needle. 'I hate mending. And I especially hate mending by lamplight.'

Through the latticework screen of the bedroom window came a chilly gust of night air. It brought the fresh damp smell of rain and it made the flame of the oil lamp tremble. The wind moaned and a distant rumble of thunder growled ominously.

Flavia squeezed her thumb and watched with grim satisfaction as a bead of blood appeared. 'That will show pater to ask me to do my own mending. Now his only child is bleeding.'

As Flavia looked up to see what Nubia's reaction would be, she caught a glimpse of herself in the new hand mirror propped up on her bedside table. It was made of tinned bronze, and was twice as big as her old one. The reflection showed a girl's scowling face. Framed by long, light brown hair, the face had a largish nose, wide mouth, and grey eyes, dark in the dim light of the oil lamp. Displeased, Flavia gave the table a nudge with her elbow and the mirror fell down with a clatter.

The noise made Nubia look up. She was sitting cross-legged on her bed, grooming her dog Nipur with a boxwood comb. 'It is better to mend in

87

daylight,' she said mildly, 'lest the needle prick you.'

'I know.' Flavia sucked her thumb. 'But I prefer to use daylight for more important things.'

'Like reading,' said Nubia, with a smile.

'Exactly,' said Flavia, pushing the needle into the hem of her tunic. 'I don't know why pater hired Aristo to teach us Greek if he expects me to spend all day doing needlework. Anyway, Alma should be mending this, not me.'

'Your pater says every Roman matron should know how to sew and weave.'

'I hate the word "matron",' grumbled Flavia. 'It sounds so old and stuffy.'

A flash of lightning briefly illuminated the room in eerie silver and black, showing two narrow beds, one with fair-haired Flavia and a golden dog, the other with dark-skinned Nubia and black-furred Nipur. From outside came a deep rumble that ended in a resounding crack of thunder.

At the foot of Flavia's bed, Scuto lifted his head to give his mistress a reproachful look.

'Don't blame me, Scuto,' said Flavia, without looking up from her mending. 'This storm isn't my fault.'

'I like rain,' said Nubia, as she worked out a burr from Nipur's smooth black fur. 'And I like storms. When you are warm and cozy inside,' she added. 'Not when you are outside.'

Suddenly Nipur sat up, growled and gave a single bark.

'Oh Nipur!' said Flavia. 'You're as bad as Scuto. You're both as timid as two old mice. There's nothing to be afraid of.' As she glanced up at him, she saw the shape of a large man filling the doorway.

Flavia gasped, then pressed her hand to her thumping heart. 'Oh, Caudex,' she said. 'You nearly frightened us to death!'

'Sorry,' mumbled the big door-slave. 'Only there's someone here to see you.'

'Someone here to see us? At this hour?' Flavia stared at Nubia in disbelief. 'And in this weather? Isn't pater back yet?'

Caudex scratched his armpit and shook his head. 'The master and Aristo are still out,' he said. 'Boy's asking for you by name. Says it's a matter of life and death.'

'Life and death?' Flavia looked at Nubia, and for the first time that evening she smiled. 'It sounds like a mystery!' Flavia put down her mending and took her wax tablet from the table. 'Mysteries always cheer me up. Come on, Nubia. Let's see what our night visitor wants.'

Caudex had left the youth dripping and shivering in the atrium. Flavia guessed he was about sixteen or seventeen. A flash of lightning through the rectangular gap of the compluvium showed his features: large dark eyes, a small mouth and a long nose in a thin face. His boots were muddy and his hooded cloak dripping. In his right hand he held a lamphorn.

'Excuse me for coming at this late hour,' he said. 'But I didn't know where else to turn. My name is Marcus Favonius Quietus and I need your help.'

'Of course,' said Flavia. 'I'm Flavia and this is my friend Nubia. Caudex, can you take our visitor's cloak and give him one of pater's from the hook?'

'What's all this about then?' Flavia's old nursemaid Alma emerged yawning from her sleeping cubicle beside the vestibule. Her hair was tied up in an orange scarf.

'Alma!' Flavia took the youth's cloak from Caudex and thrust it into to Alma's surprised arms. 'Please hang this above the hearth, to warm it? And could you make us your special poculum? Three of them? We'll be in the triclinium. No, Caudex, not that one. Give me pater's grey felt cloak. It's soft and warm. That's it. Now please light some lamps in the triclinium, and the brazier, too.'

Caudex nodded and shuffled off towards the inner garden.

Flavia handed the young man her father's winter cloak and he accepted it gratefully.

'Come,' said Flavia. 'We'll go sit in the triclinium.

There are three nice padded couches in there and Caudex is lighting lamps and a brazier. Don't mind the dogs. They won't bite. Follow me.' Flavia led the way out of the atrium and along the columned peristyle around the inner garden. The rain was beating down hard and a chilly breeze was gusting, but Caudex had just finished lighting the hanging oil lamps and the dining room looked bright and cheerful. Its frescoed walls showed the exploits of Hercules against a deep red background.

'Now,' said Flavia gesturing for the youth to sit on the central couch, 'what did you say your name was again? I'm good at clues but bad at names.'

'Quietus,' said the youth. 'Marcus Favonius Quietus.'

'Hmm,' said Flavia. 'That name sounds vaguely familiar.'

'My great-uncle came to you a few months ago. Marcus Favonius Probus.'

'I remember!' said Flavia. 'The legionary from Londinium. Did he ever find the treasure?'

'Yes. He sailed to Britannia last July and returned in September, fabulously rich. He bought the house where I live now. He used the rest of his money to buy land in the salt flats up by Portus.'

'What are salt flats?' asked Nubia, sitting on the left-hand couch and pulling her blanket around her shoulders.

'Salt flats are those marshy areas outside town,' said Flavia, sitting opposite her on the right-hand couch. 'You know the big grey cones like piles of sand we see sometimes? That's salt. My great grandfather made his fortune in salt, but he sold our land.' Flavia turned back to Quietus, who was warming his hands over a bronze tripod full of coals.

'So,' said Flavia, 'my advice helped your great-uncle find the treasure?'

'Yes, it did.'

'Hmmf. He might have thanked me!'

'He should have thanked you,' said Quietus. 'But now he cannot. He is dead.'

'Dead?' Another flash of lightning and crack of thunder from outside.

'Yes,' said Quietus. 'They found him drowned in the baths last month.'

'Oh, poor man,' said Flavia. 'Just when he should have been happy.'

'Even with wealth he could not be happy,' said Quietus. 'In fact, I think it made him more miserable.'

Alma came into the lamplit triclinium with three silver goblets on a tray. Flavia took one of the goblets, relishing the warmth against her fingers and its spicy smell of wine, cardamom and milk.

Quietus took his and began to lift it to his lips. Then he uttered a hoarse cry and the cup clanged onto the mosaic floor, splashing the steaming pink liquid. The dogs rushed forward to investigate the spreading pool.

'What's wrong?' cried Alma. 'Did you burn yourself?'

'Barley!' gasped the youth. 'There were barley grains floating on top!'

'And grated cheese,' said Flavia. 'That's Alma's special poculum. Everybody loves it. See?' Flavia gestured towards the two dogs, happily lapping up the pool of milky cardamom-spiced wine.

'But I fear barley grains,' said the youth. His teeth were chattering.

'Then I'll bring you one without barley,' said Alma kindly. 'It's no trouble.' She rolled her eyes, and disappeared into the darkness of the peristyle.

'You're afraid of barley grains?' said Flavia.

'Yes,' said Quietus, pulling her father's grey felt cloak tighter around his shoulders. 'That's why I'm here. The Barley Grains of Death.'

A flash of lightning illuminated the inner garden beyond the columns. The fig-tree, so lush and comforting in the summer, stood bare and white for a moment, then dissolved into darkness and rain. The crack of thunder came a moment later.

'The Barley Grains of Death?' echoed Flavia. She glanced at Nubia, whose golden eyes were wide.

'Yes. My great-uncle received them and died. My

93

father received them and died. And now I have received them, too.' Quietus bit his lower lip and Flavia could tell he was trying hard not to cry.

Flavia picked up her wax tablet and opened it; the stylus was inside. She held it poised. 'Tell us,' she said. 'Tell us everything. Start from the beginning.'

Quietus obediently took a deep breath. 'My family had a small pottery near the docks up by the river mouth,' he said. 'We lived in rooms above the shop where we sold our amphoras to ship-owners and merchants. My great-grandfather was a potter, so was my grandfather and my father. And so am I. It provides a good steady income, but it's not a very exciting life. My father always used to tell us tales of his Uncle Probus – my great-uncle – who dreamed of adventure. When Uncle Probus was sixteen, he joined the Ninth Hispana and was posted to Britannia where he fought blue-painted barbarians and savage warrior-queens with long red hair.'

'Boudica,' said Flavia to Nubia.

'Uncle Probus was the hero of our family: brave, adventurous, and successful. After the British rebellion, he was posted to the governor's staff in Londinium. So you can imagine my family's excitement when he reached the age of retirement and came back to Ostia with a pretty, young wife. He bought an apartment near us. It had nice rooms and a balcony with violets. He was happy at first but then his wife became ill. He spent all his money on doctors but she died. He had to sell his apartment.'

'He spent the last of his money on her tomb, didn't he?' said Flavia.

'That's right. He came to live with us for a while, but it was very crowded. Then, one day last July, he went out sad and came back happy. He said a girl named Flavia Gemina had told him where to find some treasure in Britannia. Of course we had heard of you – like everyone in Ostia – but we all thought he was mad to take the advice of a ten-year-old girl.'

'Eleven,' said Flavia. 'I'm eleven.'

'Despite our objections, Uncle Probus borrowed enough money for passage to Britannia. He sailed via Massilia and the Pillars of Hercules. Two months later he was back, with an enormous fortune in gold and silver. We were all astounded. He paid off his debts, and still had enough left over to buy a fine town house near the baths of Claudius, along with some property in the salt flats. You would have thought his riches would make him happier. But if anything he was worse.'

Quietus took another deep breath and continued.

'He began to claim he was being followed. He stopped going out. He stopped watering his wine and often became drunk. After a while, he invited me to come and live with him. I became his companion and the steward of his household. I read to him, played latrunculi, helped him to bed if he drank too much neat wine.' Quietus held his hands over the brazier to warm them. Flavia noticed they were trembling.

'One morning about six weeks ago, on the Kalends of October, a messenger brought a letter. I took it to Uncle Probus. He was sitting at the table in his inner garden, eating breakfast. The sun was shining and the birds were singing. He seemed happy for once. Then he opened the letter. Some little grains of barley fell out onto the marble tabletop. He uttered a cry and stood up so violently that his chair fell over. I started to laugh, but stopped when I saw the expression on his face. His eyes were bulging and his mouth was wide open, like one of those marble masks in the theatre. He was terrified.'

Another crack of thunder split the night, and at the same instant a brilliant flash of lightning illuminated the inner garden.

'Great Juno's peacock!' exclaimed Flavia when the thunder had died away. 'Were the grains of barley poisoned?'

'I don't think so. They were just little grains of barley. Five of them.'

'And what did the letter say?'

'Nothing.'

'What? No writing? No message?'

'Only a blue oval with a line through it. Uncle

Probus cried out: *The five barley grains! The blue theta! May the gods forgive me!'*

'Blue theta?' said Flavia.

'In the arena, theta stands for *thanatos*, which means "death" in Greek. If you put it next to a gladiator's name, it means he is dead.'

'I know that. But why blue?'

'I don't know. I asked him what was wrong and he replied: *My sins have caught me at last. I am doomed.* I begged him to tell me what it was about, but he refused. He went into his bedroom and bolted the door from inside.' Quietus shook his head and stared at the mosaic floor. 'The very next day he sent me out to find seven freeborn men and when they arrived he got them to witness a new will.'

'Do you know who his heir was?'

'It was his nephew. My father. Marcus Favonius Figulus.'

'So your great-uncle knew he was going to die,' said Flavia.

'Yes. And twelve days after he got the letter, he drowned.'

A gust of damp wind made all the lamps in the dining room flicker.

'Was it an accident, do you think?' asked Flavia. 'Or murder?'

'I don't know. Someone found him floating face down in the hot plunge of the Baths of Claudius.

The doctor said he probably fainted because of the hot steam and then fell into the pool and knocked his head and died.'

'What was the doctor's name?'

'Aristides.'

'And there were no witnesses?'

'No. Uncle Probus liked to bathe at night, when the baths were empty. He hated crowds. He paid extra to have the place to himself.'

Alma came into the triclinium with a fresh beaker of spiced wine for Quietus and a plate of honey cakes.

'Thank you, Alma,' said Flavia, and they each took a cake.

Quietus sipped his spiced wine. His hand was no longer shaking.

'So,' said Flavia, chewing thoughtfully. 'Your newly rich great-uncle Probus gets a mysterious and terrifying letter, makes his will and dies. And his nephew Figulus inherits. Your father.'

'Yes.' Quietus stared into his goblet. 'After the funeral and the reading of the will, pater and mater came to live in Uncle Probus's house with me. Pater began to take an interest in the revenue from the salt flats.'

'How many slaves did you bring with you?'

'Only mater's body slave,' said Quietus. 'But Uncle Probus left us an old Phoenician door-slave who came with the house.'

'Your parents only had one slave?' said Flavia. 'Then your family wasn't very rich?'

'No,' said Quietus. 'We were not rich. But we were happy. I know that now.'

'But then your father died.'

'Yes,' said Quietus. 'A week after the Ides of October he also received the letter with the Barley Grains of Death.' Quietus took another sip of spiced wine and Flavia saw that his hand was trembling again.

'And?' said Flavia.

The rain was coming down even harder and another flash of lightning cast them in a brief ghastly light.

'Twelve days later,' said Quietus, 'he was dead.'

The crash of thunder made them all jump.

'And the letter contained the barley seeds?'

'Yes,' said Quietus. 'Five of them.'

'And the blue theta? The sign of death?'

'Yes, it had the blue mark. But it also had a message.' Quietus looked up at the ceiling and recited: '*Sell your estate and all your possessions and leave the gold in the tomb of the Favonii three days before the Kalends of November.*'

'Great Juno's peacock,' murmured Flavia. 'I take it he didn't sell the estate?'

'No,' said Quietus. 'Pater liked the new house and his life of leisure. The appointed day came and went.

He died three days later, on the Kalends.'

Flavia made the sign against evil. 'How?' she asked. 'How did your father die?'

'He had been at the salt flats, supervising the slaves. One of the salt-gatherers found him later, face down in half a foot of water. He had been drowned, just like Uncle Probus.'

'And nobody saw it happen?'

Quietus shook his head.

Flavia took another honey cake. 'Why barley grains?' she murmured.

'Uncle Probus once told me something about being in the legion. He confessed that when he was a new recruit, he was backward at learning drills. They used to punish slow learners by beating them with a rod and giving them their grain allowance in barley rather than wheat. Uncle Probus told us that he and some of his friends were always being put on rations of barley. He said they made a joke of it.'

'What is wrong with barley?' asked Nubia. 'I like it.'

'Pliny says barley is only fit for animals,' said Flavia.

Quietus shrugged. 'I like barley, too,' he said. 'But once, when mother served barley porridge, Uncle Probus threw his bowl at the wall.'

Flavia snapped her fingers. 'Maybe a soldier killed your uncle. And the barley is a kind of insult.'

'Maybe,' said Quietus. 'But I was never in the legion so why did I receive the Barley Grains of Death? Here.' He reached into his belt pouch and brought out a piece of folded papyrus. I brought it for you to see.'

'Excellent,' murmured Flavia. She slipped off the couch and went to Quietus and took the folded papyrus. Then she sat beside Nubia and together they examined the outside of the letter.

'It's addressed to Marcus Favonius Quietus,' said Flavia. 'That's you.'

He nodded.

'The writing is very neat. Either the murderer is educated or a professional scribe wrote it. Maybe we can show this around the forum tomorrow. See if anyone recognises the handwriting.'

'Good idea,' said Quietus. 'Nobody thought of doing that.'

Flavia looked at Nubia, took a deep breath, and opened the letter. Five little barley grains pattered out onto the couch. Despite herself, Flavia shuddered. Then she read the letter.

Below a crude blue theta were words written in neat black ink:

Sell your estate and all your possessions and leave the money beside the urn of legionary Probus in the Favonius family tomb. Do this by the Ides of November or share his fate.

'The Ides of November?' cried Flavia. 'When did this come?'

'On the Nones,' said Quietus in a small voice.

'But the Ides have come and gone. Why didn't you come to me before now?'

Quietus shook his head. 'I don't know. I tried showing this to a magistrate, but he told me not to worry. Then, tonight's storm made me fearful. I had a terrible premonition.'

'You went to the magistrates?'

'Yes,' said Quietus. 'But they said it was probably just a prank. After a short investigation, they said there was nothing suspicious about the death of Uncle Probus or my father.'

'Idiots!' muttered Flavia, and she studied the note. 'I have no idea what the barley grains are,' she said. 'But your uncle told me the Britons used to daub themselves with blue paint or mud before they went into battle. This blue theta makes me think of their battle paint. I wonder ...'

'What?'

'What if the rightful owners of the treasure realised your uncle found the treasure buried on their property? What if one or more of them followed your uncle back here to Ostia? I urged your uncle to share the treasure with them, but I'll bet he kept it all for himself.' She looked at Quietus. 'Is there anyone at your house right now?'

'Just my mother. And our two slaves.'

'Your mother's all alone? Apart from her young slave-girl and the old door-slave?'

'Yes.'

'Nobody else?'

'No.'

'Great Juno's peacock!' cried Flavia. 'We don't have a moment to lose!'

She jumped off the couch. 'Your father was told to have the money ready three days before the Kalends,' she said over her shoulder. 'He didn't, and he died three days later.' Flavia was running along the dark peristyle. As she led the way into the dimly lit atrium she continued breathlessly: 'You were told to have money by the Ides and today is also three days later. The murderer could be on his way to your house right now.' She yanked her hooded cloak from the wall peg and pulled on her fur-lined boots. 'So come on!' she cried, unbolting the door.

Flinging it open, she saw two figures: one fumbling with a key, the other holding a torch.

'Pater!' she cried. 'Aristo! Praise Juno you're back. You've got to help us. Can you go and get a magistrate and some vigiles? Meet us at the house of Favonius near the Baths of Claudius? We haven't a moment to lose!'

'What in Hades?' Her father and Aristo exchanged glances, then her father saw the pale youth behind her. He shook his head and sighed. 'All right. But this had better be serious.'

'It is! It's a matter of life and death! Oh, Alma!' cried Flavia over her shoulder. 'Prepare the guest room. They can't stay a moment longer at that cursed house!'

She pushed past her father and plunged into the wet night, pulling Quietus after her. Nubia followed with the two dogs on leads, then Caudex with a flaming torch of pitch pine which threw their trembling shadows onto the wet street. At the crossroads, by the fountain, Flavia, Nubia and Caudex turned right. Her father and Aristo went straight on.

'Stay with them, Caudex,' she heard her father shout. 'Don't let anything happen to them.'

'Hurry!' said Flavia to Quietus. 'Oh dear Castor and Pollux, may we not be too late!'

The thunderstorm had passed, but it was still raining hard as they hurried up Bakers' Street. Caudex's torch made the drops of rain looked like golden arrows falling from the heavens. As they turned right onto the Decumanus Maximus, Flavia almost slipped on the wet stones of the pavement.

After the Cartdriver's Baths they turned left, then right along one of the older streets towards the Baths of Claudius. Flavia's heart was thumping and she could not shake a feeling of dread. Now Quietus led the way, with Caudex close behind.

Suddenly Quietus stopped with a grunt of despair.

'What?' cried Flavia, peering through the rain. 'What is it?'

Quietus pointed at the open door of a house further up the street. 'The front door is open! I'm sure I closed it behind me,' he said.

He ran ahead and disappeared inside. 'Mater!' they heard him cry. 'Mater!'

Caudex followed him in, brandishing his torch like a sword, so that the flames roared. The swinging torch made shadows swoop and fall in the atrium. Caudex held it up and as the flames steadied and grew brighter, Flavia screamed. A woman's body floated face down in the impluvium.

Quietus stood looking down at the figure in the pool, his arms hanging loose. Then he lifted his face to the sky. 'Praise Jupiter!' he cried, and looked at them. 'It's just a wooden statue of Fortuna that my uncle bought after he moved in. Someone must have pushed it over. Mater?' He turned towards the inner rooms and cried out again: 'Mater?'

'Marcus!' came a woman's strangled cry from somewhere inside. 'Marcus, help!'

Scuto and Nipur began to bark as Quietus plunged into the dark doorway of a corridor leading deeper into the house.

'Follow him, Caudex!' squealed Flavia, but the big door-slave was already moving off, taking the light with him. Flavia, Nubia and the barking dogs hurried after him.

In the garden courtyard, dark shapes of dripping shrubs loomed ominously. As Caudex hurried along the columned peristyle after Quietus, his torch lit a succession of theatrical masks painted on the wall. Flavia knew their staring eyes and gaping mouths were meant to avert evil, but on this dark and stormy night they were terrifying.

Suddenly a blue man burst out of the dripping shrubbery and crouched before them, ape-like.

Flavia and Nubia both screamed. The stocky man was naked apart from a coating of blue paint and a loincloth. Even his face was painted, so that the whites of his eyes stood out. Caudex swung his torch at him. The man jumped back, avoiding the flaming arc.

Then everything happened very fast.

The naked blue man feinted left, towards the screaming girls, then charged off to his right towards the entrance of the house. As he did so, he tripped over Nipur and sprawled on the wet gravel path.

In a heartbeat, Caudex had his boot on the man's neck and was shouting something in a language Flavia had never heard him speak before.

The man said nothing, but Flavia saw the gleam of white as he rolled his eyes.

Caudex spoke again, and brought the torch down low, close to the man's face.

'Get off!' cried the man in perfect Latin, and then he let loose a torrent of curses that made Flavia's cheeks grow hot.

Caudex lifted the torch away from the man's face and handed it to Flavia. She put it in a bracket on the peristyle wall. When she turned back, Caudex was hauling the man to his feet.

'Bring him over here, Caudex,' said Flavia, 'but be careful.'

Caudex nodded and shoved the blue man forward under the shelter of the peristyle.

Up close, Flavia could see he was a stocky old man; at least forty years old, maybe more.

'Praise the gods,' said Quietus, emerging from a room with his arm around a middle-aged woman: his mother, no doubt. When she saw Caudex holding the blue man she buried her face in her son's shoulder. Behind her came an old man and a young girl, both rubbing their wrists.

'Are they all right?' cried Flavia.

'Mater will be fine,' said Quietus, holding up a leather thong. 'He tied her up, and the slaves, too. He didn't hurt them, but if we'd arrived any later ...' He shuddered.

Flavia took the thong and handed it to Caudex. 'I think you'd better tie his hands,' she said.

Quietus's mother turned her head to peek at the naked blue man. Then she hid her face again and began to sob hysterically.

'Mater,' said Quietus, as Caudex tied the man's hands behind his back, 'Perhaps you and the slaves should go back to your room, while we question your attacker.'

She nodded and the three of them retreated into one of the bedrooms.

As soon as they had gone, Quietus came to stand before the blue man.

'Who are you?'

The man looked at them, his black and white eyes staring out of a bizarre blue face. Up close, Flavia could see that his hair, also plastered with blue paint or mud, was thin on top.

'You're a legionary of the Ninth Hispana,' said Flavia. 'Aren't you?'

The man turned his staring eyes at her. Then he drew himself up to attention and said. 'Lucius Celerinius Vitalis! Retired legionary of the Ninth.'

'You served with a man called Probus, didn't you?' said Flavia.

'Yes,' said Vitalis, still at attention. 'I served with Marcus Favonius Probus.'

Quietus stepped forward. 'And you murdered him, too! Didn't you?' He was trembling again, but this time with rage.

Vitalis's blue shoulders slumped. 'Yes. But it was his fault. He broke our pact.'

Flavia put her hand on Quietus's arm to calm him. 'Tell us,' she said to the blue man. 'Tell us what happened.'

Vitalis looked around at them, then licked his blue lips. 'There were five of us,' he said. 'We were young and full of blood. Always joking. We were locked up more than once, and given barley rations for showing off at drilling. One day, when we were all eating our barley, we decided to form a secret society. The Five Barley Grains. Those were good times.' He grinned.

Flavia felt Quietus stiffen beside her and she stood on tiptoe to whisper in his ear. 'I think he's mad. But we should hear him out.'

Quietus gave a single nod, but she could see the muscles clench in his jaw. 'Go on,' he said.

'Then that madwoman Boudica started the revolt. Tortured and murdered innocent men, women and children. We had orders to march and intercept. But they ambushed us. Our commander ordered us to fight. The five of us took one look at each other and knew that wasn't going to happen. We galloped off south. Pretended we were scouting ahead to warn people. We told them Boudica was coming and to hide their treasure. After they'd gone, we'd take it for ourselves. Didn't do too badly. Then one day Probus and his pal Virgil went to a smallish farm, while the three of us went to a big estate over the hill. When we joined up with them later to share the booty they said there wasn't any, but their eyes had a kind of glint. When the three of us accused them of finding something big, they denied it. But later, when one of the settlers stabbed Virgil and we were all standing round watching him bleed out, he looked at Probus and quoted some verse.'

'So Virgil didn't die in the final battle against Boudica?' said Flavia.

'No. None of us took part in that battle. We took to dressing like natives, so nobody could identify us. Smeared ourselves in blue mud, like this. Robbed houses, stole horses. Left a blue theta on the walls. It was our mark. But on one of our expeditions, a householder stabbed Virgil and we decided it was time to stop.'

Flavia glanced at Quietus, wondering how he would take the news that his adored uncle was a coward, not a hero. The young man was very pale.

'Funny thing was,' said Vitalis. 'When we turned up back at the fortress after the revolt was quelled, we became heroes. They gave us all comfortable jobs as secretaries or adjuncts. Probus was posted to Londinium, as bodyguard to the governor. I got the post of cornicularius and ended at a place called Eboracum, founded ten years after the revolt. Big

Marcus and little Marcus – the other two – they both died in the great fever of Otho, which meant Probus and I were the only surviving members of the Five Barley Grains. I soon spent my share of the booty. I kept an ear out for Probus, in case he went back for that treasure. But as he never got rich, I supposed we had all been mistaken.'

Vitalis was shivering now. Out of the corner of her eye, Flavia saw Nubia slip away, but she was too engrossed in the story to wonder why.

'Then, last August, one of my contacts on the legate's staff wrote to me. Told me that Probus was back in the country, and that he had sold some silver plate in Londinium and changed it to gold. A vast sum, they said. By the time I reached Londinium he was gone. But it was easy enough to find out he'd come back here, where he had family. I got the next ship out and when I saw how Probus was living, I was angry. We had a pact. An agreement to share everything we got!'

Nubia reappeared with a blanket and draped it around the shoulders of the shivering ex-legionary.

'So you sent him the barley grains?' said Flavia. 'But why no message?'

'I just wanted to frighten him. But then when I followed him into the baths that night he tried to attack me!'

'Were you dressed like that?' asked Flavia.

'No,' said Vitalis. 'I was dressed normally. I tried to reason with him like a civilised person. But he attacked me! We struggled and he hit his head. It was an accident!' he cried, looking around the torchlit peristyle. 'Half of this should be mine!'

'My uncle's death may have been an accident,' said Quietus. 'But not my father's death. You murdered him. And I'll see you pay for that!'

'Never!' cried the man. He writhed away, leaving Caudex holding the blanket, and he ran bellowing back towards the atrium, his hands still tied behind him.

A moment later there was a terrible echoing cry.

Flavia and the others ran into the atrium to see Vitalis on the floor, writhing in agony. A soldier with a bloody gladius crouched over him. Behind them, stood her father and Aristo and a short bald man, the magistrate no doubt.

'Pater!' cried Flavia, as she saw the pool of dark red blood spread out from beneath the blue man. A moment later her father and Aristo were beside them.

The soldier stood up and looked at the magistrate. 'I'm sorry, sir,' he said. 'I thought he was attacking you. Didn't realise he was unarmed. He ran straight onto my sword.'

Quietus went to stand over the man, oblivious to the blood pooling around his feet.

Blue Vitalis looked up at the young man and tried to speak. But all he could manage was a rattling sigh.

'He's dead,' said the soldier, rinsing his sword in the impluvium and drying it on the woolen arm of his tunic. 'I'm sorry.'

'It's probably for the best,' said Quietus. He glanced at the statue of Fortuna, still floating face down in the impluvium. 'This place is cursed. I'm going to sell it and the salt flats, too, and donate the proceeds to the Temple of Jupiter, Juno and Minerva.'

'What about you and your mother?' asked Flavia. 'And the two slaves? Where will you live?'

'Luckily, the sale of our pottery hasn't yet gone through,' he said. 'We'll go back there, where we were happy. I'll be a potter again. It may be a dull life, but at least it's an honest one.' He turned to Flavia. 'May we stay with you, just for tonight?'

Flavia looked up at her father.

'Of course,' said Marcus Flavius Geminus. 'Your slaves may stay with us, too.'

'Good,' said Quietus. 'We'll get what we need now and I'll send the slaves back for the rest tomorrow. Will you attend to this?' he asked the magistrate.

The bald man nodded.

A few moments later Flavia and the others emerged from the villa into the night. It had stopped raining. High above them, a full moon sailed through tattered clouds.

As they turned right onto the Decumanus Maximus, Quietus fell into step beside Flavia.

'Thank you for saving my life, Flavia Gemina,' he said. 'And the life of my mother, also.'

Flavia sighed. 'Don't thank me,' she said miserably. 'If I hadn't solved that mystery in July then none of this would have happened. And my theory about the murderer was totally wrong.'

'It wasn't your fault my father died,' said Quietus, 'It was my uncle's greed that caused our misery. You were only trying to help.'

'But now you have nothing,' said Flavia.

'You're wrong. I have my life and my mother and a girl named Marcia to whom I shall propose tomorrow. I have learnt it's far better to be a modest potter than a hunted rich man. No, Flavia Gemina. Thanks to you, I have my life. You have given me everything.'

— AUTHOR'S NOTE —

I adapted another Sherlock Holmes mystery – 'The Five Orange Pips' – to make this story. You can read a full account of the process at the end of this collection of mini-mysteries.

THREPTUS AND THE SACRED CHICKENS

This story takes place in October AD 81
(after the events of the final book in the
Roman Mysteries series, book XVII,
The Man from Pomegranate Street)

One mild October morning, Threptus the beggar boy sat on the beach of Ostia and looked out to sea. Two weeks earlier his idol Lupus had sailed away on a ship with a dolphin sail and he was never coming back.

Lupus was a legend among Threptus and his friends. On cold winter nights, huddled around a fire in the pine woods, they would tell each other the story of Lupus's rise from beggar to millionaire. Only three years ago, Lupus had been an illiterate beggar-boy like them, living rough in the graveyard outside the town walls. He scrounged, begged and stole food, just like them. He found bits of clothing and other trinkets on the rubbish pits among the tombs, just like them.

But unlike them, Lupus had a terrible disability: his tongue had been cut out by an evil slave-dealer and he would never talk again.

Despite this handicap, Lupus had made friends with a rich Roman girl named Flavia and her African slave-girl Nubia and a Jewish boy named Jonathan. Although the four of them were not much older than Threptus and his gang, they had rid Ostia of kidnappers and made it safe for children. They had even been sent on missions by the emperor Titus.

But now the emperor was dead, and his younger brother Domitian had sent Lupus and the others into exile. Threptus knew 'exile' meant you had to leave your country, and could never come back. That was why Lupus had sailed away on the ship with the dolphin sail. That was why he was never coming back.

Threptus swallowed hard and blinked back tears.

He cast his mind back to the day two weeks earlier, when Lupus had noticed him for the first time. It had been Lupus's last day in Ostia and he had given Threptus two commandments and a precious gift.

Threptus looked at the object his hero had given him.

It was Lupus's own wax tablet: two flat rectangles of wood hinged together with a pair of leather thongs. Inside, each rectangle had a shallow depression full of yellow beeswax. Threptus brought the tablet to his nose and sniffed. The wax smelled sweet, like honey.

Threptus picked up the bronze stylus. It was not much longer than his forefinger, and much thinner, but it was heavy for its size, smooth and cool. One end was pointed, for writing. The other end was flat, for rubbing out.

Threptus would never use this stylus or tablet; they were too precious. Lupus himself had written on the honey-scented beeswax. He had written two commandments. The first was: CARRY ON MY GOOD WORK and the second told him to: LEARN TO READ AND WRITE. Threptus knew this because Lupus's tutor Aristo had read the messages out loud.

Lupus had entrusted him with an important mission. To carry on his good work. But before Threptus could do that, he needed to learn to read and write.

For that he needed to hire a tutor like Aristo, or to attend school. And those things cost money. But he was only a poor beggar-boy, living hand to mouth.

Tears filled his eyes again and this time he let them spill over.

He carefully closed the tablet, with the stylus nestled between the two leaves, and put it back in the greasy leather belt-pouch that he had found on one of the rubbish tips outside the town walls.

Threptus hugged his knees again and gazed out at the horizon. The soft sand on the beach was still cool, but the sun was warm on his back.

How could he, a poor beggar-boy, learn to read and write so that he could carry on Lupus's good work?

What would Lupus do?

Immediately Threptus had the answer. Everybody knew that for one sestertius per week you could attend the forum school. If he could use his special sneaky beggar-boy skills to solve a mystery, then he might earn a reward. He could use the reward money to pay for a few weeks at the forum school, just long enough to learn to read and write.

All he had to do now was find a mystery and someone willing to pay him to solve it.

Threptus knew just where to start.

Although it was only an hour after dawn, Ostia's forum was already crowded. Threptus jumped up onto the base of a statue of a man on horseback, and hooked his elbow around one of the horse's painted marble legs. From this vantage point he could scan the forum for danger, which usually came in the form of an older boy named Naso. But Threptus could not see Naso's red hair anywhere.

His nostrils flared at the scent of meat from the morning sacrifices cooking on charcoal braziers. He could also smell incense from the lofty temple of Jupiter, Juno and Minerva over to his left. He could hear the jingle of a tambourine from within the Temple of Rome and Augustus on his right, probably a dedication. The bankers and money-changers had set up their tables in the shade of the colonnade and were already doing brisk business. He could hear the clink of coins and the deep bark of one of their watchdogs. A steady stream of people were making their way to the basilica; today was one of the days when cases could be heard.

Threptus nodded with satisfaction: it was business as usual in the forum of Ostia. He jumped down from the statue base and made his way to the notice board.

Threptus couldn't read, but he could eavesdrop. Most Romans read out loud, so he could just cock an ear and listen as they muttered their way through the various announcements of news: imperial edicts, court cases, births and deaths, lost and found.

Sometimes people even drew pictures of what they were looking for. Today, for example, someone had drawn a kind of eagle, or perhaps a vulture. That was strange. Vultures were not common in Ostia. In fact, Threptus had never seen a real vulture, only a fresco of one in the Temple of Isis. There was writing next to the picture on the notice board. Threptus didn't know letters but he did know numbers one through ten. And he knew the sign for a sestertius: two standing up lines connected by a short flat line next to a snake-shaped squiggle: HS. In front of the sign for sestertius were the crossed leaning lines that meant ten. So whoever found the vulture would get ten sesterces.

That was a lot of money.

Threptus held up both hands – fingers spread – and examined them. Ten sesterces was more money than he had ever had in his life. It must be a very valuable vulture.

He was trying to think where a vulture might hide in Ostia, when the sound of children chanting caught his attention. It came from one of the nearby colonnades, the one near the office of the lamplighters' guild. This was the forum school.

A few steps took him to the colonnade. The boys and their teacher met in a shady walkway between some columns and a blank wall. The lamplighters did not come to their office until late afternoon, so early morning noise did not bother them. The school was hidden from view by three rush screens propped up between the columns. The screens were like sleeping mats, only taller. Every morning at dawn, the teacher unrolled these three mats and leaned them against the columns. In this way he blocked the many distractions of the forum. The screens were tall enough to keep seated boys from seeing out, but not too tall to prevent citizens and parents from peeking over to check that all was well. Threptus padded forward on his bare feet and slowly brought his face close to one of the screens, close enough to peep through a crack between the reeds.

Ten boys, aged four to eleven, sat on stools with their backs to the smooth wall. They all had large, single leaf wax tablets on their knees. Three older men stood nearby. Threptus knew they were paedagogi. Their job was to accompany a boy to school and make sure no harm came to him. Only prosperous families could afford such a slave. Most boys had to do without.

Threptus could hear the teacher's raspy voice, but he couldn't see him, so he moved to the screen at the end of the colonnade. Now he could see him: a short, bald man with a beard like a billy-goat. His name was Lucius Furius Caper, but everyone called him by his nickname: Magister Flagellum. Master Whip. He was holding a whip at the moment. It was made of three flexible reeds bound together at one end to make a handle.

Magister Flagellum stopped the boys from chanting with an upraised hand.

'Porcius?' said Magister Flagellum in his raspy voice. 'Will you continue?'

One of the older boys nodded, and began to mumble something.

'Louder!' commanded Magister Flagellum. 'We can't hear you. When you are pleading a case or addressing a crowd you will need to enunciate.' He pronounced the last word clearly, biting off each syllable as it came out of his mouth.

But Porcius's problem was not that his voice was too soft. It was that he hadn't memorized the passage.

'What did I tell you about not doing the

homework?' said the teacher, shaking the whip so that the three reeds rattled against each other.

'I'm sorry, sir,' said Porcius. 'But one of our slaves is ill and I had to help pater this morning.'

'No excuses!' barked Magister Flagellum. 'As the eldest of us, you must set an example. Nigellus?' He turned to the tallest paedagogus.

'No!' wailed Porcius.

'Yes,' said Magister Flagellum. He looked at one of the boys. 'Postumus, hold his feet.'

Threptus felt a thrill of horror as Nigellus the paedagogus stepped forward and bent his knees. Porcius reluctantly came up behind him and put an arm over each of Nigellus's shoulders so that his elbows were either side of the man's ears and his chest pressed against the paedagogus's back. Nigellus grasped Porcius's arms and then stood up, bringing Porcius's feet off the ground. At the same time, Postumus knelt and grasped Porcius's ankles and pulled, so that Porcius was suspended at an angle in midair. Magister Flagellum nodded grimly and he pulled up the skirt of Porcius's tunic, revealing the boy's bare buttocks.

Threptus's jaw dropped as the teacher brought the three-reed whip down on Porcius's naked bottom. The whip smacked. Porcius squealed.

The whip smacked again. Again Porcius squealed and writhed in mid-air, but he was held tightly and there was no escape. The whip smacked a third time, and a fourth. Now Porcius's cries were constant, a shrill wheezing cry that made Threptus think of a piglet being chased around the farmyard.

'Ha, ha, ha,' said a voice beside him. 'That's funny.'

Threptus's stomach lurched. It was red-haired, spotty-faced Naso, the youth who had been trying to lead him into a life of crime.

Naso chuckled again, and took a bite of a round white onion. He ate onions the way most people ate apples: crunching them raw. When the schoolmaster had counted out ten, and Porcius limped back to his stool, Naso turned to Threptus.

'So, my son.' Naso hooked his arm around Threptus's neck and walked him away from the colonnade. 'Haven't seen you in a while.'

Naso was only fourteen, but he called all the members of his gang 'my son'.

'I've been busy,' stammered Threptus. He averted his eyes from Naso's unpleasant face and saw two dark-haired boys watching him. Nine-year old Quartus and ten-year-old Quintus were standing beside a statue near the message boards. The brothers had been his friends until Naso started grooming them for crime.

'Hello, Quartus. Hello, Quintus,' said Threptus.

Only a month earlier they would have grinned and

joked with him. Now the two of them stood unsmiling, their arms folded, trying to look tough.

'You owe me two weeks' dues, my son,' said Naso to Threptus. 'Quartus and Quintus have been doing real good at paying me. You not so much.'

'I know...' Threptus hung his head. 'That's because I don't like stealing things.'

'What? What's that? Speak up, son.'

'I don't like stealing.'

Naso took a bite of onion. 'Don't be stupid. You used to steal all the time. An apple here, a few nuts there... I've just increased the value of what you take. Money is better than fruit. And stealing is better than begging.'

Threptus took a deep breath. 'No it's not. The stall-keepers used to let us take fruit or nuts, but since we started stealing money from them they won't give us anything. They hate us now.'

'And you want people to like you? That it?'

Threptus nodded.

'Don't you want *me* to like you? And your little gang? Don't you want us to like you?'

Threptus looked down. 'Yes,' he said.

Naso patted his back. 'Then you need to go out and liberate a few coin pouches. You still have that knife I lent you?'

Threptus nodded again, miserably.

'Show me.'

Threptus reached into his coin purse and pulled out a small knife. It was about the size of a man's thumb, with the small bronze figure of a gladiator for a handle and a sharp iron blade that unfolded from it.

Naso took the knife and opened it. 'Now,' he said, 'I did not loan you this knife so you could clean your nails. No. It's for cutting purse strings or belts. Like this.' With a single swift movement, Naso cut Threptus's twine belt. Then held it up, along with the greasy belt pouch attached. 'See?'

'Give it to me!' cried Threptus, lunging for his pouch. 'Give me my pouch!'

'Oooh!' Naso laughed and held the pouch out of reach. 'Got something for me in here after all?' He nodded to Quartus and Quintus. The two boys stepped forward and each grasped one of Threptus's slender arms.

'No money,' said Naso, peering inside. 'Just a writing tablet.'

'No!' cried Threptus, struggling. 'Don't touch that!'

Naso pulled out Lupus's wax tablet, opened it and frowned down at it. 'What does it say?'

'I don't know,' lied Threptus, blinking back angry tears. And he added: 'You know I can't read.'

Naso tossed the tablet on the ground. 'You don't need to read if you stick with me.' He turned the pouch upside down and shook it. A few pistachio shells fell out. Naso snorted in disgust and let the pouch fall to the paving stones beside the tablet and stylus.

Then he hooked his arm round Threptus's neck again, and brought his spotty face close. 'Third hour after noon,' he said, giving back the folded knife. 'Right here by this statue. And you'd better have a nice heavy pouch with you. Or else I'll get my boys here to hold you and I'll beat you just like the schoolmaster beat that piggy back there.'

Threptus was on his hands and knees searching the cracks in the paving stones at the base of the statue when a pair of battered leather sandals appeared before him and a man's voice said, 'Looking for this?'

Threptus looked up from the sandals to see a pair of chunky calves, a grubby grey tunic and a hand holding his precious bronze stylus.

'Yes!' he said, grabbing it and putting it in his belt pouch.

'I've lost something, too,' said the man. He was plump and dishevelled. An ivy wreath on his head made him look like a sad, rabbit-toothed version of Bacchus, the Roman god of wine. 'I've lost my Aphrodite.' He nodded towards the message board. 'It's been two hours since I put that notice up and nobody's found her yet.' The man

130

took a deep breath and bellowed, 'Aphrodite! APHRODITE!'

Threptus frowned. Aphrodite was the Greek goddess of love. But it could also be the name of a woman or girl. Perhaps the man had lost his beautiful slave-girl. Or his young wife. 'What does she—'

'Shhh!' said the man. 'Do you hear that?'

Threptus cocked his head and listened. The open space of the forum was full of many noises. Apart from the chanting of children in the forum school, he could hear men arguing, the auctioneer calling, priests chanting, flutes warbling, coins clinking, fountains splashing, cicadas creaking. But no girl answering the rabbit-toothed Bacchus.

'No,' said Threptus. 'I don't hear anything.'

The man's shoulders slumped. 'Neither do I.'

Threptus tried again. 'What does she look like?'

The man gestured at the notice board: 'She's beautiful. Black hair, black eyes, worth her weight in gold to me!'

Suddenly Threptus was interested. 'Are you offering a reward?'

'Ten sesterces,' said the man. His rabbit teeth gave him a slight lisp.

Threptus thought quickly. Ten sesterces would pay off Naso and buy five or six weeks of tuition in the Forum School. 'How old is she?' asked Threptus.

'Only eight,' said the man, and wrung his hands. 'She never strays far. I think someone must have taken her.'

Threptus swallowed hard. He was eight, too. 'Where did you last see her?' He asked the chubby man.

'At home. But she often comes with me to the forum, so I thought she might have found her way here.'

Threptus nodded and tried to look wise. 'I think we should go back to your house and look for clues. Whenever I lose something I go back to the place I last saw it. I'm Threptus, by the way. I'm very good at finding things.'

'Hello, Threptus the Finder,' lisped the man. 'My name is Floridius. Aulus Probus Floridius. Soothsayer and keeper of sacred chickens. Also an orator. Also a vintner. And sometimes a poet. My home is not far,' he added. 'Just behind the temple of Rome and Augustus.'

Threptus raised his eyebrows. Floridius did not look like a rich man, but his house was in the oldest and richest part of town, and only a few moments' walk from the forum. Perhaps the man was an eccentric millionaire.

But when they reached Floridius's house, Threptus's heart sank again. It was little more than a shed occupying a piece of vacant ground between the temple and a block of wealthy town houses. In a town of brick and marble, the hut's wooden walls looked crooked and sad. It was built up against the back wall of the temple, which was probably illegal. Between one corner of the hut and the temple wall ran a low fence made of reeds, forming a kind of pen. The fence came up to Threptus's armpits. He peeked over to see a dozen chickens pecking within the enclosure.

'Is this your house?' asked Threptus.

'This is indeed my humble abode,' said Floridius. 'And those are my chickens.'

'What does that say?' asked Threptus, pointing to big red letters painted on the fence. 'Do you know?'

'Course I know. Painted it myself. It says: DO NOT STEAL THE SACRED CHICKENS OF OSTIA. IF YOU DO, MAY YOUR LIVER AND LUNGS BE MIXED UP TOGETHER; MAY JUNO CAUSE YOUR BODILY FUNCTIONS TO CEASE SO THAT YOU ARE NO LONGER ABLE TO EAT, DRINK, SLEEP, SIT, STAND, WALK OR TALK. TAKE A SACRED CHICKEN AND YOU TAKE THIS CURSE!'

Threptus shuddered and made the sign against evil.

'Come in,' said Floridius. He opened a flap of the fence and closed it after them, then picked his way through clucking chickens to the battered front door.

He fumbled in his leather satchel for a moment, then pulled out a rusty house key. A moment later, the front door of the house swung open with a squeal of hinges. Threptus followed Floridius in.

There were half a dozen chickens in here, too, and Threptus noticed a small hole in the lower wall of the house just big enough to let them in and out.

There was also a hole in the ceiling.

'Compluvium,' said Floridius, noticing the direction of his gaze. 'That's my compluvium. Haven't built an impluvium yet.'

Threptus nodded and looked around.

The hut smelt strongly of cabbage and faintly of stale wine. But it was relatively clean and bright. In the centre of the room stood a rough wooden table with two stools and a battered oak chest which acted as a bench. Over against one wall was a low cot with a horsehair mattress. Threptus could tell it was horsehair because it was torn in places and he could see the stuffing. He guessed it had been retrieved from the rubbish tip. He looked for the little girl's bed but could not see one.

Threptus frowned. 'Where does Aphrodite sleep?'

Floridius looked surprised. 'Why, outside in the pen.'

It was Threptus's turn to look surprised. 'Outside in the pen?'

'Yes, come. I'll show you.'

They went back outside, into the chicken pen. Built up against the back wall of the temple were some hen houses.

'She was in here,' said Floridius, gesturing towards the open door of one of them. 'She was feeling broody.'

Threptus stared at Floridius in dismay. 'Your daughter was living in the hen-house?'

'My daughter? What daughter?'

'Is she your slave-girl then?'

'Who?'

'Aphrodite.'

'Aphrodite isn't a person!' said Floridius in astonishment. 'She's a chicken. A sacred chicken. Worth her weight in gold.'

Threptus frowned. 'But you said she had black hair. Chickens don't have hair.'

'This one does. Hair like a cat.'

'Cats have fur.'

'My chicken has hair.'

'She does?'

'She does. Look, here's her sister: Candida.' Floridius reached into the cage and removed the strangest hen Threptus had ever seen. She was perfectly white, with exotic poufs on her head and body. She looked like one of the exotic birds from the river fresco in the Temple of Isis. Candida clucked and purred in Floridius's hands.

'Go on,' said the soothsayer. 'You can stroke her.'

Threptus reached out his hand to stroke the fluffy white hen, then drew back his hand in disbelief. 'Her feathers are like hair!' he said. He reached out and stroked Candida again. 'Soft and silky.'

'Told you.'

Candida was no longer purring. Now she was scolding. 'Bk, bk, bk...B'kak!' she said.

'Better put her back on her rock,' said Floridius.

'Rock?'

'Keeps her happy. She needs something to sit on. These are the broodiest hens you ever saw.'

'What's broody?'

'Means they love to be mothers. They'll sit on anything. Other hens' eggs, duck eggs', even smooth rocks.'

'That's not very smart,' said Threptus.

Floridius gave a rueful grin. 'My silky hens may not be smart, but they are loving and affectionate. Candida and Aphrodite are dearer to me than daughters.'

Threptus looked around the pen with its reed fence.

'Maybe Aphrodite flew over the fence,' he said. 'It's not very high.'

'Most hens don't fly,' said Floridius. 'Especially the silky ones like Aphrodite. Also, chickens stay where the food is.'

Threptus looked up into the pure blue sky. 'Maybe a hawk swooped down and took her. Or a vulture! I saw a notice in the forum. Someone was offering ten sesterces for a missing vulture.'

'I thought you couldn't read.'

'I can't. But there was a picture. I think it was a vulture. Maybe it was a hawk.'

Floridius seemed to deflate, like a full wineskin with a fast leak. 'That was no vulture. That was Aphrodite. I drew that picture.'

'Oh,' said Threptus. 'Oh, I'm sorry.'

'Don't worry. I'm better at writing than drawing. Besides,' said Floridius. 'Aphrodite was sitting on her egg, wasn't she? She hardly ever comes out of the pen when she's sitting on an egg. Or an egg-shaped rock.'

'Then someone must have come in here,' said Threptus, 'and stolen her.'

'What about my warning sign? The curse against thieves?'

'Maybe the thief couldn't read.' Threptus put his head into the coop and looked for clues. 'What does sacred mean?' he asked. His voice echoed in the small space.

'It means special. Holy. Dedicated to the gods.'

'Why are these chickens sacred?'

'Because they prophesy the future.'

'How?'

Floridius lowered his voice. 'Sometimes by their entrails,' he said.

'By their–' Threptus banged his head as he brought it out of the coop too fast.

'Shhh!' Floridius put his finger to his lips and looked around. 'We don't want to upset them,' he said, and added: 'Mostly they predict the future by eating.'

'By eating?'

Floridius nodded. 'Before a battle, a good commander always consults the sacred chickens. If they eat, that means he'll win the battle. I've been using them for court cases. To tell the lawyer whether he'll win his battle or not. They've been doing very well.'

'But aren't chickens always hungry?'

Floridius chuckled. 'Pretty much. And a good keeper will remember not to feed them before a big battle. Still, the chickens never lie. Sometimes they do refuse to eat.' Floridius picked up a normal looking hen and stroked her. 'Three hundred years ago,' he said, 'a handsome but dim-witted commander named Pulcher was about to attack some ships in a harbour at night. Everything was perfect. The enemy soldiers were sleeping. The moon lit the way. His men were full of confidence. But then the soothsayer sprinkled crumbs of honey cake on the deck of the ship, and the sacred chickens refused to eat!'

Threptus stomach growled at the mention of honey cakes. 'Maybe they were seasick,' he said.

'It was a terrible omen,' lisped Floridius. 'Pulcher's brave men were now quaking in their boots. He was so angry that he reached down and grasped one of the chickens by the neck and he said: *If they won't eat, let them drink!* Then he tossed it overboard!'

Threptus stared at Floridius for a moment, then began to giggle.

Floridius looked pained. 'It wasn't funny! Pulcher suffered a disastrous defeat. And it served him right. The sacred chickens never lie.' His eyes filled with tears. 'My Aphrodite is more than a prophet to me,' he said. 'She's my friend.'

'Then I'm going to help you find her,' said Threptus, and he dropped to his hands and knees and began to search the ground.

Almost immediately he saw something glinting in the dust. It was a tiny spherical pink bead, smaller than a grain of wheat. He glanced around and almost immediately he saw another.

So did one of the hens.

She got to it first.

'What is it?' Floridius squatted down beside him. 'What have you found?'

'Don't move!' commanded Threptus. He had just spotted something else: the print of a small sandaled foot. He stood up and placed his foot next to it. The footprint was slightly smaller than his foot, and perfectly smooth: it had been made by slippers, not outdoor shoes.

'Footprints!' exclaimed Floridius. 'Of course! Why didn't I think of that?'

Now Threptus saw another footprint. And then another. They seemed to lead from the gate to the chicken coop and back. But they were very faint, and overlaid by prints of chicken feet. Was he just imagining it? He rolled back the bit of fence that served as a gate.

No. He wasn't imagining it: there was a much clearer footprint, this one outside the fence. Floridius was behind him now, and slowly they tracked the prints across the waste ground to the back door of one of the houses behind the temple.

Floridius and Threptus stared at each other.

'Who lives there?' asked Threptus. His head tipped back as he looked up at the three-story wall.

Floridius shrugged. 'Don't know. I've never seen anyone come out of this door. A rich man, I suppose.'

'Or a rich child,' said Threptus, 'judging by these footprints.'

'Or a dwarf,' said Floridius, and gave the door a tentative push. He shook his head. 'Doesn't budge.'

Threptus pushed, too, but the wooden door seemed as solid and immovable as the wall around it. Nevertheless, the footprints led from there and returned back to it.

'Whoever stole your chicken,' said Threptus, 'is in there!'

Threptus was balancing on Floridius's shoulders, a bare foot either side of the soothsayer's head. He was trying to reach one of the lower branches of an umbrella pine that overshadowed the house with the back door.

'Edepol!' grunted Floridius. 'You're heavier than you look.'

Threptus scowled. His idol Lupus could climb trees like a monkey, but he could barely cling on to the rough bark. He should have practiced more.

'Just a little higher,' he said to Floridius.

'What? You want me to grow?'

'Can you stand on tiptoe?' asked Threptus.

'No. But try standing on my hands.'

Floridius held up his hands, a good half a foot higher than his shoulders – and Threptus carefully stepped into them. It felt strange to have his bare feet supported by someone's hands. But the extra height brought him within reach of the lower branch. He grasped it, gritted his teeth and – using more willpower than strength – he pulled himself up.

Now he could use small branches and stumps of branches to reach a single bough that extended almost all the way to a small window high in the back wall of the house.

'Are you sure you want to do this?' asked Floridius in the kind of whisper actors used on stage.

Threptus put his finger to his lips, but he gave Floridius a nod, stretched out on the branch and began to pull himself along it, like a worm on a twig. Once he glanced down, but the sight of Floridius's distant and anxious face made the world around him start to spin. He was more than two stories high.

Threptus closed his eyes and clung to the branch. After six deep breaths, the world stopped spinning. He knew not to look down again.

From the ground it had looked as if he might be able to gain access to the house through the window. But the branch would not get him close enough.

However, it did grant him a glimpse inside the house. He could clearly see part of a painted wall inside. The fresco showed a garden full of birds and flowers. He could also see the head of a narrow bed. It had a shiny blue bedspread, and a pink bolster and pillows in different jewelled colours. On the bed were three rag dolls – one big, one medium, one small – lined up neatly against the bolster. A little girl's bedroom. Could she be the thief? But why would a rich girl steal a chicken?

Threptus backed along the branch to the main trunk. Above him was the mushroom-like canopy of the tree, overhanging the red tile roof of the house by about six feet. He couldn't climb through the canopy: it was too dense. But if he swung along its lower branches, he might be able to drop down onto the roof. Carefully, he climbed higher and higher. It was nearly noon now, and hot. His hands smelt of pine resin. Above him, a cicada was creaking loudly. It stopped as he came closer to it. At last he reached the lower branches of the canopy.

'No!' hissed Floridius. 'Threptus, no! It's not worth breaking your neck for a silly hen.'

'She's not a silly hen,' Threptus muttered to himself. 'She's your friend. Besides, I need that reward money!'

He took a deep breath and swung himself out along the sturdiest-looking branch of the canopy. This wasn't as hard as climbing; he just had to swing himself forward arm to arm, like a monkey. He kept his hero Lupus in mind until he was over the roof.

For a long moment he dangled at arm's length and looked down. The roof was covered with terracotta tiles shaped like half pipes. The higher tiles overlapped the lower ones, giving the roof a look of bumpy orange-red fish scales. Threptus knew that such tiles kept the house cool in summer and warm in winter, and that they channelled rainwater to the gutters with their lion head spouts.

But as he dropped from the branch, he learnt

something new. Tiles were not made to be walked on. The impact of his feet on the tiles set them in motion and he felt himself beginning to slide down towards an inner garden far below.

He turned and tried to scrabble back up the incline of the roof. But with a terrible inevitability the sickening downward motion of the roof was gaining momentum. Threptus's arms flailed and his mouth opened to call for help. But it was too late. The tiles were slipping and he was falling.

Threptus opened his eyes to see long-lashed dark eyes only a few inches from his.

'Oh!' cried the little girl, recoiling. 'You're alive!'

Threptus propped himself up on his elbows and groaned. His legs were scratched and his bottom bone ached.

'You're lucky the jasmine bush broke your fall,' she said, sitting back on her heels. 'You could have broken your neck.' She had wavy black hair pulled back and pale skin and big eyes so dark they looked black. Her mouth was small and pink, the same colour as her long-sleeved tunic and her bead necklace. He guessed she was about his age. Perhaps a little younger.

'What happened?' he asked.

'You were on our roof and you fell down.' She picked up a broken roof-tile and examined it.

'Oh,' he groaned again as he sat up.

'Threptus!' came Floridius's faint voice. 'Threptus! Are you all right?'

'I'm all right!' he called back at the top of his lungs, and added under his breath. 'I think.'

'Is your name Threptus?' asked the girl.

'Yes.' He stood up stiffly and patted his legs and arms. Nothing broken. But he ached all over.

'What were you doing on our roof?'

He glanced down at her feet. She wore pretty pink silk slippers with smooth leather soles. Her feet were a little smaller than his.

'I was looking for the chicken you stole.'

'Oh!' Her hand went to her mouth and he saw her cheeks flush. 'Oh!'

'Arria Pollitta!' A shrill voice from the colonnade. 'What on earth are you doing in there?'

Threptus and the girl both turned. A thin young woman emerged from a shadowed corridor and limped into the sunny garden. She had dark eyes and frizzy hair scraped back into a bun. She was wearing a coarse, sleeveless tunic. In her hand she held a small wineskin.

'By Isis!' she cried, when she saw Threptus. 'Who are you? Where did you come from?' Her eyes widened as she looked from him to the battered jasmine bush and up to the roof with its missing tiles.

'Thief!' she cried. 'You're a thief!'

'No I'm not.' Threptus pointed at the girl. 'She's the thief. She stole my friend's sacred chicken.'

The woman's mouth opened, then closed, then opened again: 'Arria Pollitta?' she said. 'What is all this about? Did you steal a sacred chicken?'

'I didn't steal it. I only borrowed it,' said Pollitta defiantly. 'And you are not to tell mater. Now, give me that milk.'

The young woman limped forward and Threptus saw that one of her legs was slightly twisted. She handed the wineskin to Pollitta and glared at Threptus.

'Go!' commanded Pollitta, flapping her hand. 'Go back to your chores.'

The slave-girl snorted and limped out of the garden.

When she had gone, Pollitta turned to Threptus. 'Come with me,' she said. 'I want to show you something.'

The wooden door squeaked as Pollitta pushed it open. Threptus followed her into a dim, narrow room. It was cool in here and smelt strongly of wine, and faintly of mildew. His stomach growled again. Pollitta laughed and it sounded like the silver wind chimes in the Temple of Isis.

A small high window let in a dusty beam of light.

It illuminated an old loom leaning against one wall. As his eyes adjusted to the dim light, Threptus could see amphoras sunk into the sandy earth and shelves full of square glass jugs and round ceramic pots.

'It's our store room,' said Pollitta. She caught Threptus's hand; he let her pull him forward. Her fingers were warm and slightly moist.

Then he saw it: a fluffy black chicken with feathers as soft as hair. Aphrodite was sitting on a pile of yarn, near the foot of the loom, clucking softly. There was another sound, too. A mewing sound.

To his amazement, a little grey and black kitten pushed its head out from under Aphrodite's wing.

'Mew!' it said. 'Mew!'

'Great Juno's beard,' he murmured. 'She's hatched kittens.'

Pollitta regarded him solemnly with her liquid black eyes. 'Don't be silly. Hens don't hatch kittens.' She sat down crossed-legged on the sandy floor and lifted the kitten from beneath the fluffy black wing. Immediately Aphrodite began to fuss and cluck.

'This is Felix,' said Pollitta, nestling the kitten in the crook of one arm. 'He's the runt of the litter. Pater drowned his mother and his brothers and sisters.' She placed the nozzle of the wineskin to the kitten's mouth. 'The hen keeps him warm, and I feed him.'

'With wine?'

'No, silly! With goats milk.'

147

Threptus squatted beside her. Now he could smell the warm milk. And he could see the kitten's tiny stomach swelling. His own growled fiercely; he had not eaten since the previous day.

Behind the loom, Aphrodite was strutting in a circle, clucking to herself.

'Stroke the hen, will you?' asked Pollitta, 'Just until I finish feeding him.'

Threptus stroked Aphrodite. He was amazed at how soft and warm she was. Under his firm gentle strokes, the hen calmed down a little.

'How did you know the hen would protect the kitten?' he asked.

'Before Pater became rich he used to be a farm-slave. He told me this type of hen will sit on anything from a rock to a scorpion. When he put the kittens and their mother in a bag and took them away, I managed to save this one. I can feed him but I can't be with him all the time. But she can.'

'Aphrodite,' said Threptus. 'The hen's name is Aphrodite.'

Pollitta looked at him with her huge black eyes. 'If you take Aphrodite away, my kitten will die.'

'What happens if you father comes in and finds them?'

Pollitta hung her head. 'He'd probably eat Aphrodite.'

'Floridius says their flesh is black and doesn't

148

taste very nice,' remarked Threptus.

'Pater wouldn't mind. Then he'd probably drown Felix and beat me for disobeying his orders. And for stealing.'

'Is your father here?' asked Threptus nervously.

'No. He's in the forum.'

'And your mother?'

'At the baths with her friends.'

Threptus thought for a few moments.

'Pollitta, I used to steal things.'

She looked at him with her big dark eyes. 'You did?'

'Yes. But last month a boy called Lupus told me to carry on his good work. He gave me this.'

Threptus pulled the wax table from his belt pouch and handed it to her.

Pollitta opened the tablet. 'I can't read,' she said. 'What does it say?'

'It says: Carry on my Good Work. I want to be good like Lupus. That's why I stopped stealing.'

'I don't know who Lupus is.'

'But you know stealing is wrong.'

Pollitta nodded.

'Then will you please let me take Aphrodite back to her owner?'

Threptus was hurrying along the sunlit pavement with a chicken under one arm and a kitten down the front of his tunic when three figures stepped out and blocked his way.

Red-haired, red-faced Naso stood with his arms folded across his chest and his head cocked to one side. Behind him Quartus and Quintus took up identical poses.

'Hello, Threptus,' said Naso. 'That's a pretty chicken. Going to sell it at market? Or is it your dinner?'

'It's not mine,' stammered Threptus. 'It belongs to a friend.'

'Anyone I know?' Naso unfolded his arms and used the nail of his little finger to clean his right ear.

'No. I don't think so.' In spite of his terror his stomach growled fiercely.

Naso examined the nail of his little finger. 'I think that chicken should just about settle your debt to me.'

Threptus swallowed hard. He could run away, or he could fight. Or he could give Naso the chicken. Did he have any other options? What would Lupus do?

Naso clicked his fingers. 'Boys?'

Quartus and Quintus unfolded their arms and sauntered towards Threptus.

'Wait!' Threptus put up his free hand. 'You can take the chicken, but it's cursed!'

'What?'

'Yes, it's true.' Threptus took a big breath. 'This is a sacred chicken and if anyone steals it the god Jupiter will mix up your liver and lungs and he will stop you from going to the latrine so that you won't be able to eat or drink or sleep or sit or stand or walk ever again.'

Naso frowned and held up his hand. The brothers stopped either side of Threptus.

'You're making that up.'

'I'm not. It's true. And the same is true for me. I've taken a vow to Minerva not to ever steal again. So if you make me steal then I'll die and I won't be any good to you. And you'll die, too.'

Threptus's heart was thumping like a drum and his knees were trembling. But he couldn't let them see his fear.

'It's true!' said a man's voice. 'You touch that boy – or that chicken – and you'll die a horrible death.'

Threptus turned to see Floridius hurrying across the street, with two vigiles close behind him.

When he turned back to Naso and his gang, they were disappearing around a corner.

'This the boy who stole your chicken?' said one of the vigiles.

'No,' said Floridius. 'He's the boy who found it!'

'So, my little Aphrodite,' said Floridius a short time later. 'You've been hatching out kittens have you?'

'Just the one,' said Threptus with a grin. He felt wonderful. For the first time in his life he had stood up to the bullies. And he had got away without a beating.

Now he and Floridius were safely inside the soothsayer's hut, eating celebratory honey-cakes washed down with posca.

Aphrodite was sitting happily on Felix the kitten, who was full and sleepy from gently warmed goats' milk.

'Oh, I forgot,' said Threptus. He fished in his greasy belt-pouch and brought out a silver denarius. 'Pollitta gave this to me to give to you. She says she is sorry she took your chicken.'

'That's very honest of you,' said Floridius. He took the coin, examined it, then handed it back. 'You keep it,' he said. 'I think you earned it.'

Threptus took it back and also examined it. On one side it had a profile of the Emperor Vespasian and some writing. He could use this money for four weeks tuition at the forum school.

'As a matter of fact,' said Floridius. 'I owe you ten sesterces. That was our agreement, was it not?' He stood up, went to a shelf, took down a small pot and emptied out two silver coins and two bronze ones. Then he handed them to Threptus.

Fourteen weeks! Now he could buy fourteen weeks of schooling.

'Thank you, but–'

'But what?'

Threptus handed all the coins back to Floridius.

'Take me on as your apprentice,' he said. 'I'll help you and in return you let me live and eat with you. There's money for my room and board.'

Floridius took the coins and his eyes lit up. 'Really?' he said. 'You really want to be my apprentice?'

'Yes,' said Threptus. 'You can teach me how to read and write, can't you?'

'Of course,' said Floridius. 'And I can also teach you everything there is to know about sacred chickens.'

Threptus grinned. 'Euge!' he said.

'Eugepae!' said Floridius. 'Shall we celebrate with some more of Pistor's finest honey cakes?'

'Yes, please!' said Threptus. His stomach growled happily.

'Threptus,' said Floridius, putting an arm around the boy's shoulder. 'I think this is going to be the beginning of a beautiful friendship.'

— AUTHOR'S NOTE —

Sometimes a minor character catches the author's imagination, and demands more and more space on the page. So it was with the eight-year-old beggar-boy Threptus, who first appears in the final book of the Roman Mysteries series, *The Man from Pomegranate Street*. I hope that this short story will be the beginning of a beautiful friendship between me and Threptus ... and you, the reader!

ARISTO'S SCROLL

Acrisius (uh-*kris*-ee-uss)
Mythical king of Argos in Greece; it was prophesied that his daughter's son would kill him; Perseus did end up killing Acrisius by accident, when he threw a discus

Aeneid (uh-*nee*-id)
Virgil's epic poem about the Trojan hero Aeneas, whose descendents ruled Rome

Alexandria (al-ecks-*and*-ree-uh)
modern Alexandria in Egypt; a great port at the mouth of the Nile Delta, founded by Alexander the Great c. 331 BC; by Flavia's time it was second only to Rome in importance

aloes (*al*-oze)
succulent plant known for its skin-healing properties in ancient times

altar (*all*-tur)
a flat-topped block, usually of stone, for making an offering to a god or goddess; often inscribed, they could be big (for temples) or small (for personal vows)

amphora (*am*-for-uh)
large clay storage jar for holding wine, oil or grain

Aphrodite (af-ro-*die*-tee)
Greek goddess of love; her Roman equivalent is Venus

Apollo (uh-*pol*-oh)

Greek and Roman god of the sun, music and plague

Apollodorus (uh-pol-uh-dor-uss)

name of the supposed author of a catalogue of Greek myths called the *Library*; the real author is disputed but probably lived around Flavia's time

Artotrogus (ar-toe-*tro*-guss)

name of the 'parasite', a recurring character in Greek and Roman comedy; his name literally means 'bread eater'

atrium (*eh*-tree-um)

the reception room or hall in larger Roman homes, often with skylight and pool

Atropos (*at*-rope-oss)

one of the three Fates or Moirae of Greek mythology; she was the one who cut the thread of life; her name means 'without turning'

Augustus (ah-*guss*-tuss)

a title conferred on Roman emperors, it meant illustrious and hinted at an unbroken line of succession from the first emperor: Augustus

aulos (*owl*-oss)

wind instrument with double pipes and reeds that made a buzzy sound

auxiliary (ox-*ill*-ya-ree)

soldier in the Roman army who was not a Roman citizen; auxiliaries were often recruited abroad and formed specialised troops like cavalry and slingers

Bacchus (*bak*-uss)

Roman equivalent of Dionysus, the Greek god of wine and revelry

belladonna (bell-uh-*don*-uh)

AKA 'deadly nightshade'; a poisonous plant with dark blue berries

ben (ben)

Hebrew for 'son of'; Jonathan ben Mordecai means Jonathan son of Mordecai

Boudica (*boo*-dik-uh)

queen of the Iceni tribe who led a revolt against the Romans in Britain c. AD 60

brazier (*bray*-zher)

coal-filled metal bowl on legs used to heat a room (like an ancient radiator)

Britannia (bri-*tan*-yuh)

Roman name for Britain

Briton (*brit*-on)

one of the people who lived in Britannia before the Romans came; they spoke a Celtic language called Brythonic

bulla (*bull*-uh)

a type of amulet given to Roman children – usually boys – to protect them from evil; it was often a gold or silver ball, hence the name bulla or 'bubble'

caliga (*kal*-ig-uh)

heavy hobnailed sandals worn by legionaries; plural 'caligae'

Calleva Atrebatum (k'-*lay*-vuh at-ray-*bah*-tum)

modern Silchester in England: an iron-age and Roman settlement not far from London; there was a Roman presence here from the time of the conquest

Camulodunum

modern Colchester in England: a Celtic town which later became a Roman colony; after it was burned by Boudica it was rebuilt, but the administration of the province moved to Londinium

Castor (*kass*-tur)

one of the famous twins of Greek mythology, Pollux being the other

ceramic (sir-*am*-ik)

clay which has been fired in a kiln, very hard and smooth.

Cerialis (seer-ee-*al*-iss)

Quintus Petillius Cerialis, commander of the Ninth Hispana who suffered great losses in the fight against Boudica but became governor of Britannia in AD 71

cicada (sik-*ah*-duh)

an insect like a grasshopper that chirrs during the day

Claudius (*klaw*-dee-uss)

fourth emperor of Rome who ruled from AD 41 to AD 54; he commissioned the building of a new harbour at Portus near Ostia and befriended young Titus

cohort (*ko*-hort)

unit of men in the Roman army; each legion had ten cohorts

colonnade (call-a-*nade*)

a covered walkway lined with columns

compluvium (kum-ploo-vee-um)

the skylight or rectangular opening above the impluvium (rainwater pool) in a Roman atrium

cornicularius (kor-nik-yoo-*lar*-ee-uss)

officer in the Roman legion in charge of administrative work

cryptoporticus (krypt-oh-*port*-ik-uss)

Greek for 'secret corridor'; an underground passageway, usually vaulted

cura ut valeas (*kyoor*-uh oot vah-*lay*-ass)

Latin for 'Keep well!'

dactylic hexameter (dak-*till*-ik hecks-*am*-it-er)

The meter of epic poetry such as the (Greek) *Iliad* or the (Latin) *Aeneid*; it is composed of six (hex) feet (meter) of dactyls or spondees

daub (dob)

mixture of mud, dung, straw, horse-hair etc applied to wattle wall to fill gaps

Decianus (dek-ee-*ah*-noose)

procurator in Roman Britain at the time of Boudica's revolt; he botched the rescue mission of Camulodunum, sending only two hundred men

Decumanus Maximus (dek-yoo-*man*-uss *max*-i-muss)

the main road of Ostia, running from the Roman Gate to the forum

denarius (den-*are*-ee-us)

small silver coin worth four sesterces

detectrix (dee-*tek*-triks)

female form of 'detector', someone who uncovers things: detective

Diana (Artemis in Greek)

virgin goddess of the hunt and of the moon: Roman version of Artemis

Domitian (duh-*mish*-un)

the Emperor Titus's younger brother, is thirty-one years old when this story takes place

Durobrivae (dur-oh-*breev*-eye)

modern Water Newton in Cambridgeshire, England: site of a vexillation fortress which probably housed cohorts of the Ninth Hispana Legion

Eboracum (eb-or-ak-um)

modern York in England: a Roman town founded in AD 71 when a fort was built on the River Ouse for the Ninth Hispana Legion

ecce! (ek-eh)

Latin exclamation being 'look!' or 'behold!'

edepol! (*ed*-uh-pol)

exclamation of surprise based on the name Pollux: 'by Pollux!'

Ephesus (*eff*-ess-iss)

perhaps the most important town in the Roman province of Asia (Turkey)

euge! (*oh*-gay)

Latin exclamation meaning 'hurray!' or 'bravo!'

eugepae! (*oh*-gay-pie)

Latin exclamation meaning 'hurray!' or 'bravo!'

eureka! (yoo-*reek*-uh)

Greek for 'I've found it!' (pronounced 'heureka!' in ancient Greek)

Flavia (*flay*-vee-a)

a name, meaning 'fair-haired'; Flavius is another form of this name

Floralia (flor-*all*-yuh)

ancient Roman festival dedicated to the goddess Flora, it was held late April to early May and often celebrated with dancing, flowers and processions

Fortuna (for-*toon*-uh)

Roman goddess of good luck and success

forum (*for*-um)

the civic centre of Roman towns, usually an open space surrounded by shady colonnades and official buildings

freedman (*freed*-man)

a slave who has been granted freedom, his ex-master becomes his patron

fuller (*ful*-lur)

launderer who used urine, mud, chalk and sulphur to whiten wool and linen

garum (*gar*-um)

sauce made from the fermented entrails of salted fish, popular with Romans

gladiator (*glad*-ee-ate-ur)

man trained to fight other men in the arena, sometimes to the death

gladius (glad-ee-uss)

Latin for 'sword', especially the short thrusting sword of the legionary

Hades (*hay*-deez)

the underground Land of the Dead, in Greek mythology

haruspex (*ha*-roos-pecks)

priest who interpreted omens by inspecting the entrails of sacrificed animals

Hebrew (*hee*-brew)

holy language of the Old Testament, spoken by (religious) Jews in the first century

Hercules (*her*-kyoo-leez)

very popular Roman demi-god, he was worshipped by sailors in particular

Iceni (eye-*seen*-ee)

a Brythonic-speaking tribe which lived in the region of modern Norfolk in Britain

Ides (eyedz)

thirteenth day of most months in the Roman calendar (including February); in March, May, July, and October the Ides occur on the fifteenth day of the month

impluvium (im-*ploo*-vee-um)

a rectangular rainwater pool under a skylight (compluvium) in the atrium

intaglio (in-*tag*-lee-oh)

a design carved into a gem or other material

Isis (eye-siss)

Egyptian goddess who become popular with Romans in the first century AD

Italia (it-*al*-ya)

Latin word for Italy, the famous boot-shaped peninsula

Jerusalem (j'-*roo*-sah-lem)

capital of the Roman province of Judaea, it was destroyed by Titus in AD 70, eleven years before this story takes place

Juno (*jew*-no)

  queen of the Roman gods and wife of the god Jupiter

Jupiter (*jew*-pit-er)

  king of the Roman gods; together with his wife Juno and daughter Minerva he forms the Capitoline triad, the three main deities of Rome

Kalends (*kal*-ends)

  The Kalends mark the first day of the month in the Roman calendar

latrunculi (lah-*trunk*-yoo-lee)

  lit. 'little bandits' – an ancient Graeco-Roman board game of strategy, played with black and white markers on a grid, similar to checkers or chess

Laurentum (lore-*ent*-um)

  village on the coast of Italy a few miles south of Ostia

LEG VIIII HISP

  abbreviation for the Ninth Hispanic Legion (VIIII was more common than IX); a legion first created about a hundred years before these stories take place, it suffered badly in the rebellion of Boudica

legionary (*lee*-jun-air-ee)

  soldier in a Roman legion; they had to be Roman citizens

Locusta (lo-*koos*-ta)

  notorious female poisoner from Gaul who helped kill several emperors and would-be emperors, she was given an estate by Nero as thanks for helping him

Londinium (lun-*din*-ee-um)

  modern London; the Roman settlement at the first bridgeable place on the River Thames

Marsyas (*mar*-see-ass)

    Mythical satyr who challenged Apollo to a music contest and was hung from a pine tree and skinned alive when he lost

Massilia (muh-*sill*-ya)

    modern Marseilles; an important seaport in Greek and Roman times

mater (*ma*-tare)

    Latin for 'mother'

matron (may-trun)

    a married Roman woman, with a sense of dignity and respect

Medusa (m'-*dyoo*-suh)

    mythical female monster with a face so ugly she turned people to stone

Melpomene (mel-*poh*-men-nay)

    one of the nine Muses from Greek mythology; she was the muse of tragedy

Minerva (m'-*nerv*-uh)

    Roman equivalent of Athena, goddess of wisdom, war and weaving

Muse (myooze)

    one of the nine mythical daughters of Zeus and Mnemosyne; each is the patron goddess of an art or science, e.g. Clio is the Muse of history

necropolis (n'-*krop*-oh-liss)

    Greek for 'city of the dead': the graveyard, usually outside the town walls

Nero (*near*-oh)

(AD 37–68) notorious emperor who was reported to have strummed his lyre while Rome burned in the great fire of AD 64; he ruled from AD 54–68

Nones (nonz)

7th day of March, May, July, October; 5th day of the other months

oscillum (oss-ill-um)

a decorative marble or clay disc hung from eaves or between columns; they were usually painted or carved and were probably intended to avert evil

Ostia (*oss*-tee-uh)

port about 16 miles southwest of Rome; it is Flavia Gemina's home town

Otho (*oh*-tho)

Emperor who ruled for a short time in the year AD 69

Ovid (*ov*-id)

Publius Ovidius Naso; famous Roman poet who lived about 70 years before Flavia

paedagogus (*pie*-da-gog-uss)

male slave or freedman who took boys to and from school; a kind of bodyguard; plural 'paedagogi'

palla (*pal*-uh)

a woman's cloak, could also be wrapped round the waist or worn over the head

papyrus (puh-*pie*-russ)

the cheapest writing material, made of pounded Egyptian reeds

Parasite (*pare*-uh-site)

Greek for 'alongside food','someone who eats at your table'; a man or woman who relies on others to support and feed them; a stock character in Roman comedy

pater (*pa*-tare)

Latin for 'father'

patrician (pa-*trish*-un)

a person from the highest Roman social class

peristyle (*perry*-style)

a columned walkway around an inner garden or courtyard

Perseus (*purr*-syooss)

Mythical hero who had to cut off Medusa's head with a special sword and reflective shield

Pillars of Hercules

ancient Roman term for the Straits of Gibraltar, the place where you pass from the Atlantic Ocean into the Mediterranean Sea

Plautus (*plow*-tuss)

Titus Maccius Plautus (c.254–184 BC) a famous Roman playwright who wrote comedies with recurring characters such as Artotrogus, the Parasite

Pliny (*plin*-ee)

AKA 'Pliny the Elder', author of the *Natural History*; he died in the eruption of Vesuvius in AD 79

Pluto (*ploo*-toe)

god of the underworld, he is the Roman equivalent of Hades

Pollux (*pa*-lucks)

one of the famous twins of Greek mythology, Castor being the other

Portus (*por*-tuss)

harbour a few miles north of Ostia, built by Claudius to handle the increasing volume of shipping coming in and out of Rome's port

posca (*poss*-kuh)

a refreshing drink made by adding a splash of vinegar to water, very popular among legionaries; the vinegar makes even bad water safe to drink

Pulcher (*pull*-kur)

Publius Claudius Pulcher, a Roman commander who threw the sacred chickens into the sea when they refused to eat before an important battle; he lost the battle

quadrans (*kwad*-ranz)

tiny bronze coin worth one sixteenth of a sestertius or quarter of an as (hence quadrans); in the first century it was the lowest value Roman coin in production

Salvete! (*sal*-vay-tay)

Latin for 'hello!' to more than one person

satyr (*sat*-ur)

mythical creature of the woods, in Roman times depicted as a man with goat's ears, tail, legs and horns

scroll (skrole)

a papyrus or parchment 'book', unrolled from side to side as it was read

Seneca (*sen*-eh-kuh)

AKA Seneca the Younger, a philosopher who wrote about how to die a good death

sesterces (sess-*tur*-seez)

more than one sestertius, a brass coin

sestertius (sess-*tur*-shuss)

a brass coin, singular of sesterces

signet ring (*sig*-net ring)

ring with an image carved in it to be pressed into wax and used as a personal seal

stylus (*stile*-us)

a metal, wood or ivory tool for writing on wax tablets

stola (*stole*-uh)

a long tunic worn mostly by Roman matrons (married women)

Surrentinum (sir-wren-*teen*-um)

Ancient Roman wine from the region around Surrento on the Bay of Naples; it was a white wine, and quite vinegary

Surrentum (sir-*wren*-tum)

modern Sorrento, south of Vesuvius: site of the Villa of Pollius Felix

tablinum (tab-*lee*-num)

the study of a Roman house, where scrolls and writing materials were kept

Thalia (thal-yuh)

one of the nine Muses from Greek mythology; she was the muse of comedy

Thamesis (tuh-*may*-siss)

Latin for Thames, the river that flows through London

thanatos (*than*-uh-tows)
Greek for 'death'

theta (*they*-tuh)
eighth letter of the Greek alphabet, it resembles an oval with a dash inside; represents the 'th' sound

Titus (*tie*-tuss)
Titus Flavius Vespasianus died on 13 September AD 81, after ruling as emperor for just over two years; he was forty-one years old

toga (*toe*-ga)
a blanket-like outer garment, worn by freeborn men and boys

triclinium (trick-*lin*-ee-um)
ancient Roman dining room, usually with three couches to recline on

tripod (*try*-pod)
a bowl, usually bronze, on three legs, hence the name tripod; often used as braziers

tunic (*tew*-nic)
a piece of clothing like a big T-shirt; children often wore a long-sleeved one

Tyrrhenian (tur-*ren*-ee-un)
sea to the west of Italy, named after the Etruscans

Verulamium (vare-yoo-*lame*-ee-um)
(modern St Albans) Romano-British town in Hertfordshire; it was destroyed by Boudica in AD 61

Vespasian (vess-*pay*-zhun)
father of Titus and Domitian and emperor from AD 69 to AD 79

vestibule (*ves*-t'-byool)

the antechamber of a Roman house, usually leading into the bigger atrium

Vesuvius (vuh-*soo*-vee-yus)

volcano in Naples which erupted in August AD 79

vexillum (vecks-*ill*-um)

(Latin for 'little sail') it was a square banner held on a pole; a vexillarius was a standard-bearer and a vexillation fortress a fort that housed half a legion

vigiles (*vij*-ill-aze)

the policemen/firemen of ancient Rome; the word means 'watchmen'

Virgil (*vur*-jill)

AKA Publius Vergilius Maro, a famous Latin poet who died in 19 BC, about a hundred years before this story takes place

wax tablet

a wax covered rectangle of wood used for making notes

wattle (watl)

a fence or wall woven with branches of hazel, willow, or other flexible wood

HOW FANS HELPED ME
WRITE A MINI MYSTERY

In the introduction to this book, I explained why *The Legionary from Londinium* is a collection of short stories rather than Roman Mystery XVII. I also explained about my idea that Flavia could be 'an armchair detectrix' and solve a mystery set in Britannia without leaving Ostia. That story was *The Legionary from Londinium*. I also thought it would be fun to 'adapt' the Sherlock Holmes mystery story that first gave me the idea of having Flavia solve an 'armchair' mystery, 'The Five Orange Pips' by Sir Arthur Conan Doyle. As with 'The Lion's Mane', I thought it might be fun to do a Roman version. Of course Flavia would be the detective, not Sherlock Holmes, and it would be set in first century Rome, not Victorian London. I could keep the basic structure but I would have to change the details.

For example, 'The Five Orange Pips' begins in a typically verbose Victorian fashion:

> *It was in the latter days of September, and the equinoctial gales had set in with exceptional*

> *violence. All day the wind had screamed and*
> *the rain had beaten against the windows, so*
> *that even here in the heart of great, hand-*
> *made London we were forced to raise our*
> *minds for the instant from the routine of life*
> *and to recognise the presence of those great*
> *elemental forces which shriek at mankind*
> *through the bars of his civilization, like*
> *untamed beasts in a cage. As evening drew in,*
> *the storm grew higher and louder, and the*
> *wind cried and sobbed like a child in the*
> *chimney. Sherlock Holmes sat moodily at one*
> *side of the fireplace cross-indexing his records*
> *of crime, etc, etc . . .*

You get the idea.

If I wanted to rewrite that opening in the style of *The Roman Mysteries*, I could do something very simple . . .

> *It was a dark and stormy night in the Roman*
> *port of Ostia, and Flavia Gemina was in a*
> *bad mood.*

I could make the English names Roman and the American origin of the mystery Britannia. Now all I needed was something to stand in for the orange pips. The Romans didn't really know about oranges.

I wanted something much more Roman. But what could it be?

In March 2008, I gave a talk at the Museum of London, explaining two of my methods for writing stories. I told my listeners that I wanted to make a Sherlock Holmes mystery story Roman. I explained how I would do it. Then I asked them to look round the collection of Roman artefacts in the museum and send me their suggestions. Something that could 'stand in' for orange pips. The person who came up with the best clue would be the winner. They would get their name in my book of short stories, and the whole collection would be dedicated to them too!

Runners-up would get a signed copy of this book. Fans came up with some great suggestions.

AISLING: five grape seeds from grapes used to make wine

CLARE: gold coin of Fortuna holding a rudder which was paradoxically cursed

CLEMENT: blue glass beads, once belonging to Boudica

EMILY: five fish-scales from a poisonous African fish that only Nubia recognises

OTANA: five barley seeds, a mark of disgrace among soldiers

SANNE: five mosaic pieces, each with a letter which makes a secret message

SARAH: part of a jewelry set, the letters on the jewels spell Boudicca

SEBASTIAN: five human teeth from a murder victim

VERA: a strand of Boudica's hair which points to her murderer

VICTORIA: five scraps of papyrus (the mystery comes in the form of a letter from Britannia)

Some ideas for artefacts which could be clues to a different sort of crime included:

ALEXIA: a gladiator's trident, a murder weapon

CONNIE: an iron strigil, used to cut off Lupus's ear from behind

CONNER: a Roman spoon with traces of poison on it

DAVID: a coin broken in half each half given to twins separated at birth

ELIZABETH: a green glass bottle, which held deadly poison

EMILIE: a statue, when you turn its hand a trap door opens, leading to captured children

GIGI: a goblet, with traces of dried blood showing it was used as a weapon

HARRY: ten hairpins, found in the river Thames: murder weapon (ouch!)

HELEN: forged Roman coins (forging currency was a serious crime in Roman times)

HELENA: an iron brooch depicting a dog, stolen from the Emperor Titus

JONATHAN: a jewel, the only clue left from a murder/robbery

JOSHUA: a mosaic, from a burned villa

LIBBY: pieces of lead waste (mined in the Mendip Hills) used as a blunt instrument

ROSA: iron slave chain and shackle, the murderer strangled someone with it

SUSIA: brooch of hunting dog, which means 'I'm hunting you, murderer'

TATIANA: theatrical mask, it comes alive in Flavia's nightmare and is Pluto

THEO: a ring, which says 'Curse your riches, Titus'

ZACHARY: a hammer with dry blood on it, attempted murder weapon

I love all the suggestions, but in the end I went for Otana's five barley grains. Although barley grains aren't strictly an artefact, there are some ancient Roman barley grains in the Roman exhibition at the Museum of London. Also, Otana didn't just suggest the barley grains and leave it there. She gave me two pages of back-up research, citing Roman authors like Vegetius, Polybius and Pliny the Elder. She told me why barley grains would be a good substitute for orange pips. For example, soldiers who were bad or clumsy at drill were often punished by having their allowance given in barley rather than wheat. It was a public disgrace for a soldier to receive barley rations.

I decided to use Otana's idea and I hope you like the result.

A big thanks to Otana, who gets all the kudos, and to the three fans who get honorable mentions and a signed copy of this book – Rosa, Helen and Zachary.

Thanks also to curator Jenny Hall from the Museum of London. Next time you visit it – or any other museum – keep an eye out for likely clues to a mystery!

Caroline Lawrence

Have you read . . .?

TRIMALCHIO'S FEAST
AND OTHER MINI-MYSTERIES

Some careful readers of the Roman Mysteries ask Caroline Lawrence questions like 'Who is Porcius?' or 'What happened with the monkey at Lupus's ninth birthday?' or 'Will we ever find out what happened to Silvanus from *The Colossus of Rhodes*?'

Caroline even plants clues in the books to be fleshed out in other stories. At the beginning of *The Enemies of Jupiter*, Jonathan makes a reference to the disaster that was Lupus's birthday party. Caroline says, 'I purposely put that in before I wrote "Trimalchio's Feast" knowing that there wouldn't be a book set in February AD 80 but that I didn't want to leave Lupus out and have no one know when his birthday was.'

This first collection of mini-mysteries will help fill some of the gaps in the books and answer some of *your* questions.

Have you read . . . ?

FROM OSTIA TO ALEXANDRIA
WITH FLAVIA GEMINA

Join Caroline Lawrence on a behind-the-scenes tour of the exotic locations which have inspired the Roman Mysteries. With this guide, plan your own travels following Caroline's insider tips and top advice for a memorable family holiday.

Read about famous sites and little-known places in this collection of diary extracts, traveller's anecdotes, fact files, excerpts from the novels, and Caroline's own stunning colour photographs.

See if you can carry out the tasks in each of the places visited, and learn more about the inspiration behind your favourite characters.

Places featured:

ITALY
Ostia, Rome and the Bay of Naples

GREECE
Athens, Rhodes, the Greek islands and mainland Greece

AFRICA
Morocco, Egypt and Libya